✶RICHARD PAUL EVANS✶

SIMON & SCHUSTER

NEW YORK  LONDON  TORONTO  SYDNEY  NEW DELHI

Simon & Schuster
1230 Avenue of the Americas
New York, NY 10020

First Simon & Schuster hardcover edition October 2012

SIMON & SCHUSTER and colophon are registered trademarks
of Simon & Schuster, Inc.

For information about special discounts for bulk purchases, please contact
Simon & Schuster Special Sales at 1-866-506-1949 or business@simonandschuster.com.

The Simon & Schuster Speakers Bureau can bring authors to your live event. For more
information or to book an event, contact the Simon & Schuster Speakers Bureau at
1-866-248-3049 or visit our website at www.simonspeakers.com.

Designed by Davina Mock

Manufactured in the United States of America

1   3   5   7   9   10   8   6   4   2

Library of Congress Cataloging-in-Publication Data

Evans, Richard Paul.
A winter dream / Richard Paul Evans. — 1st Simon & Schuster hardcover ed.
          p.     cm.
1. Adult children—Family relationships—Fiction.   2. Family-owned business
enterprises—Fiction.   3. Forgiveness—Fiction.   I. Title.
PS3555.V259W56   2012
813'54—dc23                               2012032646

ISBN 978-1-4516-2803-6
ISBN 978-1-4516-2805-0 (ebook)

# ✦ ACKNOWLEDGMENTS ✦

his book came to me at a difficult time. I would like to thank all those who helped me through it, beginning with my long-suffering and beloved wife, Keri, who dealt with my daily stress and middle-of-the-night panic attacks. Thanks to my daughter and talented writing assistant Jenna Evans Welch for her constant brilliance; my agent, Laurie Liss; and my editor, Trish Todd, for her patience and valuable coaching. Also, my friend, and copy editor, Gypsy da Silva—let's hit Little Brazil next time I'm in New York.

I'm grateful for the ongoing support of my publisher—Simon & Schuster, specifically Jonathan Karp, Richard Rhorer and Carolyn Reidy.

On the home front, a big thanks to the rest of the family—David Welch, Allyson, Abigail, McKenna and Michael. Also, my assistant Diane Elizabeth Glad, Barry Evans, Heather McVey, Doug Osmond and Karen Christoffersen.

A special thank you to my dear friend Karen Roylance

for her encouragement and support at a critical time in this book's development.

I would also like to thank the fine people at Leo Burnett Chicago—a true Humankind agency—who lived up to their stellar reputation in every way. I could not have chosen a finer agency to base my story around. I hope you all enjoy the book. More specifically, a special thanks to Leo Burnett's Tina Stanton and Kim Kauffman for welcoming me to your home and the tour of the Leo Burnett facilities.

I also wish to thank the infamous Bill Young for showing me Chicago in all her splendor.

*✶ To my brothers: David, Scott, Mark, Boyd, Van and Barry ✶*

# A Winter Dream

Now Israel loved Joseph more than all his children, because he was the son of his old age: and he made him a coat of many colours.

And when his brethren saw that their father loved him more that all his brethren, they hated him, and could not speak peaceably unto him.

And Joseph dreamed a dream, and he told it his brethren: and they hated him yet the more.

And he said unto them, Hear, I pray you, this dream which I have dreamed:

For, behold, we were binding sheaves in the field, and, lo, my sheaf arose, and also stood upright; and, behold, your sheaves stood round about, and made obeisance to my sheaf.

And his brethren said to him, Shalt thou indeed reign over us? or shalt thou indeed have dominion over us? And they hated him yet the more for his dreams, and for his words.

And he dreamed yet another dream, and told it his brethren, and said, Behold, I have dreamed a dream more; and behold, the sun and the moon and the eleven stars made obeisance to me.

And he told it to his father, and to his brethren: and his father rebuked him, and said unto him, What is this dream that thou hast dreamed? Shall I and thy mother and thy brethren indeed come to bow down ourselves to thee to the earth?

*And his brethren envied him; but his father observed the saying.*

*And his brethren went to feed their father's flock in Shechem.*

*And Israel said unto Joseph, Do not thy brethren feed the flock in Shechem? come, and I will send thee unto them. And he said to him, Here am I.*

*And he said to him, Go, I pray thee, see whether it be well with thy brethren, and well with the flocks; and bring me word again. So he sent him out of the vale of Hebron, and he came to Shechem. . . .*

*And Joseph went after his brethren, and found them in Dothan.*

*And when they saw him afar off, even before he came near unto them, they conspired against him to slay him.*

*And they said to one another, Behold, this dreamer cometh.*

*Come now therefore, and let us slay him, and cast him into some pit, and we will say, Some evil beast hath devoured him: and we shall see what will become of his dreams.*

—Genesis 37,
King James Version

# PROLOGUE

*Life is the soil, our choices and actions the sun
and rain, but our dreams are the seeds.*

✦ Joseph Jacobson's Diary ✦

My name is Joseph Jacobson, though most call me by my initials, J.J. For better or worse, I've also been called a dreamer. I take this as a compliment. I've always been fascinated by dreams. Both kinds: the kind we create with our hearts and the kind that come to us in the night when our mental gates are unlocked and unguarded.

Throughout history, dreams have been a source of wonder to humanity. Some of the world's greatest authors, musicians, scientists and inventors have credited dreams with revealing ideas that have changed the world.

Some believe that dreams are the very secret to understanding life. Others, like the ancient Toltecs, believed that life itself *is* a dream.

The story I'm about to share with you begins with a dream. *A Winter Dream.* One night I dreamt of myself walking through a dark, snow-blanketed forest. I came upon a tree covered with brilliant, colorful lights—like a Christmas tree. Surrounding the tree, in a perfect circle, were eleven other trees.

Then, a great storm arose. Snow whited out all the forest except for the illumination of the one tree. When morning came and the wind stopped, the eleven trees were bent, bowing toward the tree of light.

Whether the dream was prophetic or the cause of all that happened, I'll never know. But for years I kicked myself for telling the dream to my father, who, for reasons I still can't understand, chose to share it with my eleven brothers.

# CHAPTER

## *One*

*Today I had my first big break. Funny term that. Only in business and theater is a break a good thing.*

✦ Joseph Jacobson's Diary ✦

I'm twenty-nine years old and the twelfth of thirteen children—twelve boys and one girl. My father was married three times before he married my mother, Rachel. Only my younger brother, Ben, is my full brother. Growing up, he was the only one of my brothers I was close to.

My father was a better businessman than he was a family man. He's the founder and president of Jacobson Advertising, a successful Denver marketing firm specializing in retail advertising. If you've seen the Ski Heaven campaign for Vail, Colorado—the one where all the skiers have glowing halos—that was one of ours.

My father was not only the President and CEO of the agency, but the main creative force as well, garnering enough awards to cover the walls of our agency. Dad had that rare ability to cut right to the heart of consumer desire, divining what people really wanted and were buying. That's not as simple as most people think. Most people don't know why they buy the things they buy.

My father's given name is Israel, but his friends call him Izzy. Or Ace. My father is an American hero. Before he was a successful adman, he was a decorated Air Force pilot during the Vietnam War—the first American conflict where living Medal of Honor winners outnumbered the dead. My father was one of them.

All thirteen of his children, including my sister, Diane, worked at the agency. I suppose the agency was my father's way of keeping the children from three broken marriages together. I started as a copywriter, working under my stepbrother Simon, a taskmaster who thrived on impossible deadlines. I spent most of my time writing brochures and radio commercials for our smaller accounts. At that time, my father was still president of the agency, but he'd begun spending less and less time at the office to travel with my mother, leaving the company management in the hands of my eldest brother, Rupert—the agency's general manager.

My stepbrothers were, understandably, loyal to their mothers—Leigh, Billie, and Zee Jacobson (all of them kept my father's name)—and resented all the time my father spent with *my* mother. My mother was younger than my father by more than twenty years, beautiful and, as he often said, "the love of his life," which pleased Ben and me, but grated on my stepbrothers' feelings. On more than one occasion I had heard my stepbrothers refer to my mother as "the trophy," when I was too young to know that it wasn't meant as a compliment.

My stepbrothers' jealousy extended deeper than their feelings toward my mother. My father had spent the early years of my stepbrothers' lives working, building the agency at the expense of their childhoods. Only later in life, with his agency established, did my father begin to enjoy the fruits of his labors, which included spending more time with those still at home—my younger brother, Ben, and me. I really did understand their resentment, but it still didn't make my life easier.

If I had to pick a day to start my story, I'd peg it at three years earlier on the Friday morning we pitched the Dick Murdock Travel Agency—a Denver-based travel company and one of the top-twenty travel agencies in America. Perhaps it was a test, but for the first time since he'd started the agency, my father sat on the sideline, leaving the pitch totally in his boys' hands.

Sitting in on the pitch meeting were my brothers, Rupert, Simon, Judd, Dan, Gage, my father and me. On the opposite side of the table from us were three executives from Murdock: the tour coordinator, Bob; the marketing director, Marcia; and the president and company namesake, Dick Murdock, a barrel-chested man who wore ostrich-skin boots and a Bolle tie.

Our conference room had a table large enough to seat sixteen and the walls were decorated with the scores of awards we'd won, nearly all of them bearing my father's name. We dimmed the lights, and on a pull-down screen we projected our proposed slogan.

## Dick Murdock Travel
*We'll get you there*

Murdock's silence screamed. Finally, Marcia, a tall, thin woman with spiky black hair, said, "I don't get it."

Simon raised the lights. "We'll get *you* there," he said, taking on the tone of a radio announcer. "It's a powerful phrase. Travel is a matter of trust. Your clients want to know that their families, their employees and they, themselves, are in good hands. No matter where they're going, Dick Murdock Travel *will get them there*, safely, on time, on budget."

His explanation was met with more silence. I glanced over at my father. He sat expressionless. This was a man who could maneuver a jet while surface-to-air missiles were shot at him—a crash-and-burn pitch was nothing.

"Where are you getting the 'safely, on time, on budget' part?" Bob asked.

Simon squirmed a little. "It's implied."

Bob nodded slowly, the way people do when they have no idea what you're talking about but really don't care to hear an explanation.

Rupert stepped in. "Let's face it, for the business person, travel is exhausting, a necessary evil, a means to an end. Our end is getting them there so they can do what they really went to do."

Crickets.

Murdock glanced at his two employees, then sat up in his seat. "There's no zing," he said bluntly.

After a moment Rupert said, "That's just our first concept." He nodded to Judd.

Judd stood. "Like Rupert said, travel is a necessary evil, getting from A to B. So I created a play on that principle."

### Dick Murdock Travel
*From A to Z*

More crickets.

Judd continued, "From Arizona to Zimbabwe, from Alaskan Cruises to the San Diego Zoo, from the Amazon to Zambia."

"Where's Zambia?" Bob asked Marcia facetiously.

Murdock said nothing. Worse. He looked annoyed.

"Too much like the amazon.com logo," Marcia said. "From A to Z. It's been done."

Judd looked blindsided. "We've created a television spot," he said meekly.

"Don't bother," Murdock said. "I'm not sure we're broadcasting on the same frequency." He turned to Rupert. "Unlike you, we don't think of our business as a 'necessary evil.' From what I've heard so far, you'd think we were torturing our clients for a price."

"That's certainly not the message we intended to convey," Simon said.

"Intent is irrelevant, it's what's perceived that matters. And that's what I heard," Murdock said. "Travel is evil." He turned to my dad. "Is that the best you've got?"

I could only imagine what was going through my father's mind. *Mayday, Mayday, we're going down. Pulling the eject cord.* My dad looked at Simon, who looked more angry than dejected. Then he turned to Rupert. "Is that our best?"

Rupert glanced at my father, then said, "Actually, we have one more concept we want to show you. It's a bit unconventional."

"Unconventional?" Murdock said.

For Rupert, "unconventional" was a polite way of saying "out there." Three days earlier I had had a dream of a suitcase bouncing around with excitement. The words came to me, *Pack your bags!*

Rupert turned to me. "J.J., show Mr. Murdock your idea."

Truthfully, I hadn't planned on sharing my idea. When I had shared my dream with Simon, he gave me that "nice try, kid, now get me some coffee" look. Every eye in the room fell on me. I lifted my portfolio and walked to the front of the conference room. I cleared my throat.

"I'm kind of new at this, so bear with me."

"Nowhere to go but up," Murdock said.

Simon's jaw tightened.

"When *I* think of travel, I think of having fun—seeing exciting places, seeing people I care about. I think of the excitement and anticipation of getting ready. When I went to Italy a few months ago, I spent six months preparing for just ten days. So, to me, travel is more than just the time away from home, it's the anticipation leading up to it . . . like Christmas. The fun of Christmas is the preparation, the secrets and wrapping and decorating. So I came up with this."

## Dick Murdock Travel
*Pack Your Bags!*

The slogan was inset over a cartoon drawing of a travel trunk plastered with colorful stickers from different countries.

Marcia nodded encouragingly. "Pack your bags."

Bob also nodded. "I like that. I like the trunk. It's iconic. We could use it on brochures, TV commercials, tour signage, Facebook, even luggage tags." He looked at me. "What about electronic media?"

"Like Rupert said, my idea is a bit unconventional," I said. "But when the competition zigs, you should zag. Since almost all travel commercials are really just video travel brochures, in order to stand out, I think we should create a campaign with a decidedly unique look—something different than what your competition is doing or has ever done. I envisioned our Pack Your Bags travel trunk reproduced in clay animation excitedly bouncing around. Then it falls open and something representative of one of your destination pops out, like the Eiffel Tower, or Big Ben . . ."

". . . a pyramid for our Egypt tours," Bob said, catching the vision.

"Or a gong for China," said Marcia. "Or a panda."

"No one's done it before," Bob said to Murdock.

"Isn't that clay animation really expensive?" Murdock asked.

"It can be, but the bouncing effect is extremely simple and we're producing doughnuts: the opening and closing of the spots will always be the same, just the middle needs to be changed, so for one spot it's more expensive, but for three or four spots it will actually cost less than what you're currently spending on production."

Murdock looked pleased. "I like the sound of that. I like the idea. All of it." He turned to my dad. "Holding out on us, Ace? Or just setting us up with the bad stuff first?"

"It was all good," my dad said. "It just wasn't right for you. But I agree, I like the Pack Your Bags concept." He looked at me and nodded approvingly.

"All right," Murdock said. "What's next? Where do we start?"

Rupert clapped his hands together and leaned forward. "If you're ready to sign on, we'll sit down with Marcia and Bob and go over your promotional schedule and then we'll get to work."

"Make it so," Murdock said. He stood, followed by the other two. "Keep me in the loop." He turned and looked at me. "What's your name?"

"Joseph."

"Good work, Joseph." We shook hands. Then he turned to my father. "How's that pretty little wife of yours?"

"Rachel's doing great."

"She's a beautiful woman. For the life of me I don't know what she sees in a dusty old codger like you."

"That makes two of us," my dad said.

Murdock smiled. "See you on the course, Ace."

On her way out Marcia said to Rupert, "Give me a call this afternoon and we'll work out our scheduling."

"Happy to. Thank you."

They walked out of the room, escorted by Simon and Rupert. As I gathered up my things, I looked over at my father. His smile was lit with pride.

# CHAPTER

*Two*

*It is the nature of the beast—even the best
intentioned surprises sometimes go awry.*

✦ Joseph Jacobson's Diary ✦

An hour after the pitch meeting my father called me into his office. He was sitting back in a burgundy leather chair behind a massive desk handcrafted from burled walnut. He was still wearing a proud smile.

"Sit down," he said.

"Yes, sir," I said, taking one of the chairs in front of his desk.

"I'm getting too old for this," he said.

"Too old for what?"

"The dog and pony show. It used to be you could bring in a new client based on reputation alone. Today we have to create the whole campaign. How many thousands of dollars did we spend on that commercial they never even looked at," he said, shaking his head. "We would have lost Murdock if it wasn't for you."

"It wasn't just me. Everyone had a—"

He held up his hand. "Don't contradict me."

"Sorry, sir."

"I know Murdock. If he hadn't been an old golf buddy of mine, he would have hightailed it out of there the second he saw that first slogan. The three of them had mentally exited until they saw your idea. You brought them back to the table." He stood, walking over to a crystal decanter sitting on a credenza. "Want something to drink?"

"No, thanks."

He poured himself a scotch, then carried his glass back over to the desk. "You have talent. You're going to take this company far."

"You've already taken it far," I said. "And the brothers have sailed it well."

"Yes, they have. I couldn't be more proud of my sons." His gaze settled on me. "Especially you."

Parents aren't supposed to have favorites and the wise ones never admit to it, but I never had any doubt that I was my father's favorite. Unfortunately, he didn't hide it. And with eleven other brothers, being the favorite wasn't necessarily a good thing.

"Are you bringing Ashley to the celebration tonight?"

"Yes, sir."

As soon as Murdock had left our office, my father had announced a special celebratory party at our favorite restaurant, Giuseppe's.

He nodded. "Nice girl. Pretty."

"Thank you."

As usual, I wondered what he really thought of her. Throughout my dating years my father had always been closemouthed about my relationships and I honestly had no idea whether or not he approved of Ashley and me. Then again, with his track record, maybe he just thought it best to not offer romantic advice.

"She is pretty," I said. "And sharp as a tack."

"So, where are you going with that?"

"I think we're getting close."

He raised his eyebrows. "Close?"

"I've been looking at rings."

My father showed no emotion, but nodded. "Do you love her?"

"I wouldn't be looking at rings if I didn't."

"Does she love you?"

The question threw me a little. "I think so. She's told me she loves me."

"Does she mean it?"

I didn't know how to answer his question. "How do you really know that?"

He looked me in the eye. "You'll know when you don't have to ask." The gravity in his face dissipated. "But I'm probably not the best one to advise on this subject."

"You got it right eventually," I said.

A subtle smile crossed his face. "Yes, I did." He took another drink. "Enough of that. I just wanted to say congratulations and make sure you're planning on attending the celebration tonight."

"Of course. Wouldn't miss it for the world."

"Good. Good." He sat back down. "Because I have a very special surprise for you." He had a huge smile on his face.

"A surprise? What is it?"

"You do understand the concept of a surprise, right?"

I grinned. "Sorry."

He took another drink, his gaze never leaving me. "Get out of here. You've got a lot of work to do. I'll see you tonight."

"Okay." I stopped at the door. "I love you, Dad."

"I love you too," he said. "See you."

I walked out of his office wondering what he had in store for my surprise. I hoped it wasn't anything too demonstrative. Not that I wouldn't appreciate the gesture; I just didn't want to deal with the backlash of my brothers' envy.

# CHAPTER

## *Three*

*Tonight my father gave me a gift I didn't deserve.*
*I mean that in the best and worst possible ways.*

✦ Joseph Jacobson's Diary ✦

Giuseppe's was our family's official restaurant of celebration, an upscale Italian restaurant near the corner of 17th Street and Champa, where we held graduation and engagement parties, and our annual company Christmas party, which we'd had six weeks earlier.

There were thirty-two of us that night, our six nonfamily employees, the brothers and Diane, and our spouses and dates. Only Diane and Benjamin came alone.

Although my father was in a jovial mood, I was feeling a little tense, still wondering what he had planned.

Ashley noticed my tenseness and rubbed my neck. "Are you okay?"

I frowned. "There's just been a lot of stress at work lately."

"But you won the account. You don't have to worry anymore." I must have still looked anxious because she leaned forward and kissed my cheek. "I'll tell you what. We'll have our own celebration next week. I'll make a special dinner for just the two of us."

"It's a deal," I said, hoping to drop the subject.

"In the meantime, let's have fun. There's good food, good wine . . ."

". . . a beautiful girl . . ." I interjected.

She smiled. "A beautiful girl who loves you. Tonight you're the conquering hero. This is a good night. Relax and enjoy the moment."

"You're right," I said. *"Carpe diem."*

*"Carpe diem,"* she echoed.

As the evening waned and the music and Chianti took effect, the tension eased, giving way to laughter. Even Simon, the toughest on me of all the brothers, looked happy. With the brothers relaxed, I also relaxed.

After the tiramisu and coffee had been served, my father tapped his wineglass with his spoon. When the room quieted, he stood and raised a glass of red wine. "I'd like to make a toast." My father turned toward me. "A few days ago your brother Joseph shared a dream with me."

*He couldn't possibly be considering sharing . . .*

"Joseph dreamt of a tree in a dark forest, covered with colored lights—like a Christmas tree. The tree was surrounded by eleven other trees. Then a storm arose, whitening out all the forest except for the brilliant lights of the Christmas tree. When the storm was over, all the other trees were bowing toward the tree of light."

I furtively glanced around the room, seeing the stunned expressions on my brothers' faces, who clearly understood the symbolism before my father needlessly explained it to them.

"Maybe what we saw today was exactly what Joseph dreamed." He turned back to me. "Joseph shined in there. He saved the pitch. I'd like to raise a toast to Joseph. The shining tree in the forest."

His request was met with silence. Ashley squeezed my hand. My mother looked at me and smiled. I forced a smile in return, but inside I felt sick. Couldn't he foresee how they would respond? Couldn't he see what was going on around us? The brothers were already near breaking beneath the weight of their jealousy, and my father just kept throwing on more tonnage.

Only the nonfamily employees, and my mother, Ashley, Ben and Diane raised their glasses. The tension was searing. After a moment my mother looked up at my father. My father's expression hardened. He looked around at his sons, his stern gaze falling last on his firstborn, Rupert. "Is there a problem?"

Rupert looked around before saying, "No, sir. There's no problem." He looked at the other brothers, then raised his glass. "To J.J. For saving the day."

The brothers reluctantly raised their glasses. Only Simon didn't raise his glass. He sat motionless, staring at me. Then, under Rupert's gaze, he lifted his as well, slowly, like he was raising an anchor.

"One more thing," my father said. He set down his glass, then stooped down and took something from a bag behind him and lifted it up. It was a leather coat. He looked at me. "I think this will fit you now."

It wasn't just any coat. It was my father's Navy flight jacket from Vietnam—decorated with the colorful patches from his deployment, including the infamous Tonkin Gulf Yacht Club patch and the insignias of the fighter squadrons deployed on the aircraft carrier.

Everyone, including me, just gaped. I remember the first time my father showed it to me as a small boy. Even then I was awestruck, as mesmerized by its colorful patches as its history. It was something the family held in reverence like a holy artifact. I had assumed it would be passed down to the oldest child for generations.

"Fit me?" I said.

My father's eyes were moist. "I want you to have it."

The room went completely silent.

"I can't think of a better way to show you how proud I am of you." He carried it over to me. "Here, let me help you put it on."

"Dad . . ."

"Go on," he said.

With everyone watching, I hesitantly slid my arms through the sleeves and shrugged it on, the stiff, pungent leather hanging heavily on my shoulders.

"I don't deserve this," I said.

He stepped back to look at me. "It looks good. You're the same size I was at your age. I was about your age when I was deployed."

"I don't know what to say."

"Say thank you."

"Thank you."

"All right," my father said. "Back to the celebration."

I sat down, still wearing the jacket, trying to ignore my brothers' gazes. Each of the brothers stared hatefully at me, each feeling his own personal betrayal, his own jealousy and loss. I honestly didn't blame them. I'm sure I would have felt the same way. I just had no idea how deep their hurt was, or what my father's gesture would set in motion.

# CHAPTER

*No matter the roughness of the sea, Ashley is the anchor to which I've secured my heart.*

✦ Joseph Jacobson's Diary ✦

The rest of the evening was about as festive as a train wreck. The brothers and their wives cleared out as quickly as they could without being overly obvious, with the exception of Simon, who grabbed his wife and stormed out just minutes after my father's presentation. I wanted to leave too, desperately, as did Ashley, but my mother and father kept us there until the last. It was after midnight when I dropped Ashley off at her apartment. It had been a long, silent ride from the party, and Ashley just held my hand, unsure of what to say. I walked her to her doorstep.

"Do you want to come inside?" she asked softly.

"No. I'm tired."

"I understand." She leaned forward and kissed me. "I'm sorry about tonight. That was awkward."

"You think?"

She grinned. "Yes, I think."

"I just don't get how my father could do something like that. Telling the dream was painful enough, but the coat . . ."

"He just wants to show you how proud he is of you." She

leaned in closer. "Like I am." She kissed my face. "Come inside."

I exhaled slowly "Sorry. I'm just . . . *miserable.*"

She leaned back, groaning her displeasure. "All right. I understand."

"I never should have told my dad about the dream. Maybe I'm to blame. What did I hope to gain from that?"

"You're not to blame. How could you have known that he'd share it?"

I shook my head. "I don't know. But it was stupid."

"Maybe," she sighed, "but it's over. Everything's going to be okay. They'll get over it. Even Simon. I bet by Monday everything will be back to normal."

"You don't know my brothers," I said. "This hurt runs deep."

"Then it's their problem, not yours."

"Their problems are my problems."

"No, they're not. *Their* problems are *their* problems and *your* problems are *your* problems. You've got to stop carrying other people's problems."

"It's just hard. I care about them."

"Sometimes I think you care too much."

"You say that like it's a bad thing."

"Sometimes it is."

"Do I care too much about you?"

She grinned. "You can't care too much about me."

"I thought so."

We kissed again. "You sure you don't want to come inside? I'll give you a backrub."

"That sounds good. But it's late. I told my parents I'd drive them to the airport in the morning. They're leaving at six."

She groaned. "Masochist. There you go again, suffering for others."

"Okay, I admit it. I'm a pathetic pleaser."

"Where are they going?"

"Phoenix. One of their golf trips."

"I'm glad someone's having fun."

"He's earned it," I said. "I'll call you when I get back from the airport."

"All right," she said. "And don't forget about our celebration next week."

"What day?"

"Any day's good. You decide."

"How's Tuesday?"

"Tuesday's good. We'll celebrate then."

"That is if my brothers don't kill me on Monday."

"They'll be over it. And you'll be in a better mood for our celebration."

"As long as it's just the two of us."

"You can count on that." She leaned forward and this time we kissed at length. When we parted, I said, "I love you."

"I know. *Ciao*, sweetheart. Don't forget dinner at my parents' on Sunday."

"I'll pick you up at six."

"*Grazie.*"

I opened her door and she went inside. As I walked to my car, I thought, no matter how bad things were, at least I had Ashley. And nothing could come in the way of us.

# CHAPTER

*There can be no betrayal without trust. So should we not trust? No, to do so is a betrayal in itself.*

✳ Joseph Jacobson's Diary ✳

Not even five hours after laying my head on my pillow, I was up again, dressed and ready to drive my parents to the airport. I don't know why Ben didn't drive them, or why my parents hadn't asked him to. He did, after all, still live at home. He would have driven, of course, if my dad made him, but the truth is, I think they just wanted to see me.

The Denver International Airport is an amazing edifice but so far from civilization it should have its own area code. Or language. Even without traffic it took us forty-five minutes to reach the airport.

The greatest controversy in Denver involves neither sports nor politics. It's the giant blue horse statue at the Denver airport. *Blue Mustang*, by artist Luis Jiménez, is 32 feet tall and weighs more than 9,000 pounds. It has frightening, glowing, red electric-bulb eyes and is anatomically correct, which is also frightening. The statue is guaranteed to strike terror in the hearts of all travelers, which, considering how many people fear flying, makes me wonder what committee approved the beast's creation.

The horse not only looks like one of the cursed four stallions of the Apocalypse, it has lived up to its frightening image by killing its own maker. Shortly before its completion, Jiménez was killed by the statue when its head broke off and fell on the sculptor.

Since its erection in 2008, the horse has been given many names, including: Demon Mustang, Denver's Blue Curse, Old Blue, Zombie Horse, Blucifer, the Pale Horse of Death, and Apocalyptic Steed, to name a few.

From the beginning, the Colorado community has protested the horse, though state law requires that it remain for a minimum of five years. Still, a Facebook page was created to hurry its demise. There was even a haiku competition. The winning entry and my personal favorite was:

*Enormous eyesore*
*Gives a silent horse laugh to*
*My fear of flying.*

In the early morning's dim light the horse's eyes glowed eerily red. Looking back, perhaps I should have considered it an omen.

"That thing's a monstrosity," my mother said. "What was the artist trying to say?"

"Maybe he was just trying to get attention," my father said. "Like an adman. If so, he succeeded."

"There's more to life than attention," my mother said.

"You would know, sweetheart," my father said. "You would know."

My mother was the constant recipient of male attention, something that both flattered and frightened my father.

I sided my Honda Pilot up to the Delta terminal's curb and put it in park. My father climbed out first, signaling a skycap over to the car. A meaty, mustached fellow quickly obliged. "May I help you with your bags, sir?"

"Yes," my father said. "We have two bags to check."

"How many are traveling?"

"Two of us."

"May I have your IDs, please?"

My father handed him his license, then turned back to my mother. "Rachel."

"Sorry," she said. She got her license out of her purse and handed it to the skycap, who took the licenses over to his counter. A minute later the man returned with luggage tags and two boarding passes. "Two tickets to sunny Phoenix," he said. "I was just there last week. You and your daughter are going to love it."

"She's my wife," my father said.

"There goes the tip," the man said, but, obviously a pro at his job, added, "Well done, sir."

My father grinned. It wasn't the first time the mistake had been made. It wouldn't be the last. While my father was ri-fling through his wallet for a tip, my mother leaned forward and hugged me. "I love you."

"I love you," I said. "Have a good time."

"We will." She looked at me for a moment, then said, "I know last night was hard. But take it in the spirit it was in-tended. He means well."

"Okay."

"Take care of Ben."

"I always do," I said.

My dad walked up to us. "Here you go," he said to my mother, handing her back her license. "Let's go."

"Have a good time," I said.

"Of course we will. And you keep busy."

"Of course we will," I said.

He gripped my shoulder. "See you soon, son." Then he put his arm around my mother and the two of them walked into the terminal. I climbed back into my car to drive home and get some sleep.

Sunday was a day of rest, which I was grateful for. Around six o'clock I met up with Ashley for dinner at her parents' house. It was a quiet evening that ended with our making home-made ice cream and watching *60 Minutes* with her father, who fell asleep during the last segment.

Monday morning we had our usual nine o'clock staff meeting. Thankfully, none of the brothers said anything to me about the party. Not that they had forgotten—I was sure they hadn't. We were just busy. With my father gone, we were all loaded down with as much work as we could handle. In addition to the typical maintenance our accounts required, like printing and media purchases and placement, we also had the entire Murdock campaign to produce. I was glad to focus on my work.

The following Tuesday afternoon I was in my zone, writing radio scripts for the Pack Your Bags campaign, when

Simon buzzed me in my office, interrupting my concentration. "We need to see you in the conference room."

"I'm in the middle of writing," I said.

"We can't wait," he said sternly and hung up.

*We?* I hated being interrupted in the middle of my writing, but with all the tension in the office I wasn't about to fight him on this. I got up and walked to the conference room.

I was surprised to find the room filled with all of my brothers; Rupert, Simon, Levi, Judd, Dan, Nate, Gage, Ashton, Isaac, Zach and Ben.

Everyone wore grim expressions. All of the tension in the room seemed focused on Ben, whose eyes were red and puffy.

"What's going on?" I asked.

For a moment no one spoke, then Rupert leaned forward, knitting his fingers together. "We have a problem."

"What kind of problem?" I asked.

"Actually, Ben has a problem," Judd said.

I looked at Ben. "What's going on?"

Ben was unable to speak.

"I'll help him out," Simon said. He glared at Ben. "Ben embezzled from the agency."

It took a moment for the words to settle. I looked at Ben in disbelief. "You what?"

"I was going to pay it back," Ben said softly.

Ben worked in the firm's accounting department along with Dan and Judd.

"Six months ago," Rupert said, "Ben secretly transferred a significant sum of money to his bank account. Dan caught it."

"Transferred?"

"He stole it," Judd said.

I looked at Ben. "How much did you take?"

He looked at me through tear-filled eyes. "Thirty-six thousand."

"Thirty-six thousand?"

"I'm sorry," Ben said.

Rupert slowly shook his head. "Four years ago we could have just swept this under the rug and let Dad discipline him."

"Not that he would," Simon interjected.

Rupert looked at him, then continued. "But that's four years ago. Today we're a publicly traded company. We're going to have to act on this."

"*Act?*" I said. "What do you mean?"

"We're going to prosecute him," Simon said.

I looked around at them in astonishment. "You can't prosecute your own brother. They'll send him to prison. He's family." They were unmoved by my plea. "He's your brother."

"Our *brother* stole from us," Dan said.

"He's *your* brother," Gage said.

"You can't send him to prison," I repeated.

"What would you have us do?" Rupert asked.

I looked at them. As much as they had always disliked Ben and me ("Rachel's spawn," they secretly called us), they had pretty much left Ben alone, which I had always assumed was because Ben didn't receive as much attention from Dad as I did.

"How much of the money do you have left?" I asked Ben.

He grimaced. "None."

"What did you do with that much money?" I said.

"Little Benny has a gambling problem," Simon said.

I just stared at Ben for a moment, then I took a deep breath. "I can get the money." I had some and I knew my mother would help, which, indirectly, meant my father would be helping pay back the money stolen from his own company.

"It's not that simple," Simon said. "A crime has been committed. You want us to just cover it up?"

"You'll have the money," I said. "No harm, no foul."

"No harm?" Levi said. Up to that point he had been sitting back with his arms crossed at his chest. "Really, that's your answer? Benny put us all at risk. He risked our agency's reputation and especially Dad's. Had he not been caught by one of us, he would have been caught by the auditors, then it would have hit the fan. Rupert probably would have been fired and we all would have been guilty by association." He looked spitefully at Ben. "He needs to be punished."

Ben looked even more terrified.

"There's got to be something we can do," I said.

The room fell silent and I noticed that several of the brothers looked toward Simon. After a half-minute or so, Simon said, "There might be a deal to be made."

Simon glanced over at Rupert, who was looking more upset than the others. "Ben, leave the room," Rupert said.

Ben looked up, his eyes darting back and forth between his accusers.

"Go," Simon said. "The *men* need to talk."

He glanced at me fearfully as he walked out. Gage shut the door behind him.

Rupert said, "Before we called you and Ben in, we took a vote. Nine voted to turn Ben in to the authorities. But Simon had an idea." He gestured to Simon. "Simon . . ."

Simon turned to me with thinly veiled hostility. "Here's the deal, brother. Someone's got to pay. You want Ben saved—you pay the price. You quit the firm, move out of town, we'll sweep this under the rug and little Ben keeps his freedom."

I looked at him in disbelief. Then the others. They all wore the same grim expression. "You're kidding, right?"

"Dead serious," Judd said.

"Where am I supposed to go?"

"I have a contact with an agency in Chicago," Simon said. "They've agreed to give you a shot."

"You already found me a job? Premature, aren't you?"

"You tell us," Simon said.

I didn't know how to answer. After a moment I asked, "What about Dad?"

"We'll take care of Dad," Dan said. "The deal is, you're not allowed to speak to him or your mother."

Simon said, "We'll tell Dad that you wanted to spread your wings and took a job with a big-city firm."

"What if I refuse?"

Simon shook his head. "We make the call, little Ben goes

to jail. Who knows, the judge might be lenient. Maybe he'll just get a few years in a medium-security facility. Not too bad for what he did, except you know how fragile little Benny is. I give him a fifty-percent chance of surviving prison. But even if he does, he's a man with a record."

*Ben would never survive prison. He used to melt down every year at summer camp. My mother had to drive up and bring him home.*

"Your choice," Dan said. "You go to Chicago or Ben goes to prison. Either way works for us."

"So this is your play to get rid of me," I said.

"Why would we want to do that?" Simon said. ". . . Dreamer." He lifted a paper. "I have your resignation conveniently typed up. It just needs your signature."

I looked at him coldly. He had me and he knew it.

"What's the company?" I asked.

"The famed Leo Burnett," he said. "You can thank me later. Who knows, you might even make something of yourself."

"When do I have to leave?"

"Tomorrow afternoon before Dad and Rachel get back," Simon said. "We'll book the flight. No phone calls, no goodbyes. If Dad finds out what happened, the deal's off."

"If Dad finds out, he won't press charges," I said.

"When the stockholders find out, he'll have to."

"You really think they'll believe I just took off for a new life without speaking to them?"

"They'll believe it when you do it," Gage said.

He had a point. "What about Ashley? Is she just supposed to pick up her life and leave as well?"

Dan said, "If she loves you, she'll follow you. If she doesn't, then we've done you a favor."

"What do I tell her?"

"Nothing," Simon said. "If you're smart."

"Tell her you found a better offer," Judd said.

I looked back down at the paper. "Who do I talk to at this agency?"

"The creative director is Peter Potts," Simon said. "But my friend's name is Timothy. He's the one who got you in."

"I need time to find a place to live."

"We found you a place," Dan said. "It's close to work."

"You had this all planned out," I said.

"Consider it a courtesy. All you have to do is sign the resignation."

I looked at Rupert. I had always admired him. When I was young, he and his wife would sometimes tend Ben and me while my parents went out. We always had a good time. I thought that he, of all the brothers, would not go along.

"This is what you want?" I asked.

He looked pained but nodded.

My heart ached even more.

"Don't forget," Levi said, looking at Simon. "He can't take Dad's coat."

"That's right," Simon said. "That's part of the deal. The coat stays."

"It would be an insult," I said.

"Benny's rip-off is an insult," Judd said.

"The coat stays," Simon said. "No discussion." He handed me a pen. "Sign."

After years of envy and resentment the brothers finally had their revenge. As I hovered over the paper, I realized that there really was no other choice.

I signed my instrument of surrender.

# CHAPTER

## *Six*

*Someone has grabbed the wheel of my life and steered me over a cliff.*

✦ Joseph Jacobson's Diary ✦

As I walked out of the conference room, Ben was leaning against a desk, waiting for me. He looked as anxious and eager as a defendant awaiting the jury's verdict.

He stood. "What's going to happen?"

"They're not going to turn you in," I said.

He looked as puzzled as he was relieved. "They're not?"

"No."

"Why? What happened?"

"I made a deal," I said.

"What kind of deal?"

"The kind I can't tell you about."

"Why not?"

"If I do, the deal's off. So don't ask, unless you want to go to prison. Understand?"

He just looked at me blankly.

I exhaled. "I won't be around for a while."

"Where are you going?"

I stopped outside my office. "I said, don't ask. Ever."

He was silent a moment then said, "What have you done?"

"What had to be done. I made a deal with the devil. Devils."

"You can't take the hit for me."

"I already have. Now do me a favor."

"Anything," he said.

I looked him in the eyes. "Grow up."

# C H A P T E R

## *Seven*

*The greatest falls—of towers and hearts—happen
when beliefs are built upon assumptions.*

✦ Joseph Jacobson's Diary ✦

I felt like I had stepped out of that conference room into a Salvador Dalí painting. Time was bent. Everything was surreal.

I got a box from the supply closet, then went to my office and packed my things. There was no point in finishing the copy I was writing. There was no point in finishing anything. *I* was finished.

As I cleared out my desk, Rupert's secretary, Grace, delivered an envelope with my flight information, apartment lease and a severance check for three thousand dollars, presumably to help me get started. I noticed that the check was signed by Rupert, not Dan, as my paychecks were. I guessed he probably did this on his own to lessen my troubles. Or soften his guilt.

On my way out of the office I gave my sister, Diane, my office key. She was understandably confused.

"What are you doing?" she asked.

"Ask Simon," I said. "He'll be happy to tell you."

My flight was scheduled for the next day. I drove to my apartment and packed everything I could carry in two suitcases.

There were far more details than I had time to resolve. I'd have to leave my apartment for Ben to rent out. Actually, he could just move into my apartment. He was looking for a new place and had always liked mine. He could also take my gym membership. He'd have to sell my car.

As I was making out my list, my cell phone chirped, signaling that the battery was nearly dead. I plugged in the charger, then realized the futility. I would have to get rid of it anyway. It was either that or forever ignore my mother and father's calls. I might as well have been planning my own funeral. In a way I was. Life, as I knew it, was over.

I finished packing my bags, then drove to Ashley's apartment for dinner. The entire drive, I puzzled over one question: *How would I tell Ashley?*

I had been with Ashley longer than any girlfriend I'd ever had. We'd met three years earlier at a photo shoot for a brochure I'd written. At the time, she worked as a receptionist for Uphill Down, a ski parka producer and client of ours. She was strikingly beautiful, so I wasn't surprised when the president of the company asked her if she'd like to model some of their coats for their winter catalog.

The first time I saw her, she was wearing an all-white ski parka with matching snow pants and a white fox fur hat, all sharply in contrast to her onyx black hair, Windex blue eyes and bright, cherry red lipstick. Seeing her was practically a religious experience. The heavens parted and angels sang. It was love at first sight.

Ashley was born in Colorado and had lived in the Denver suburb of Thornton her entire life. She had graduated from CU in newspaper journalism. Unfortunately, Colorado's newspapers were faring about as well as the rest of the country's paper journals, and with the fall of one of Colorado's biggest newspapers, the 150-year-old Pulitzer-winning *Rocky Mountain News*, she ended up first working as a waitress at an Olive Garden, then receptionist, then model. She wouldn't be eager to move. A year earlier when I suggested she could pursue her dream of a journalism career if she applied to jobs outside of Colorado, her response was simply, "That's not going to happen." Now I had to tell her we were moving.

I knew Ashley well enough to know that I couldn't tell her the real reason we had to move. She'd never understand.

And she was headstrong. I knew what she'd do with the real story—she'd go straight to my father. I had no doubt about this. Ben wasn't a favorite of hers. She believed that he was coddled by my parents, and more than once she had expressed her opinion that he needed to suffer the consequence of his actions. I doubted that she would sacrifice living in Colorado for him.

I wasn't even sure that she could. She was one of those people who held to justice like a life ring. It's not that she wasn't merciful. It's just that her need for justice was a whole lot stronger than her desire for mercy.

On the way to her apartment I stopped to pick up some wine for dinner. We were going to need it. Tonight was supposed to be a celebration. She had even made one of my favorite dishes, spaghetti carbonara. I had been looking forward to the evening since Friday. Now I wished it were over.

Ashley smiled as I walked in. As usual, she looked stunning. Her hair was pulled back and she wore a tight black dress, her tiny waist accented with a purple sash. She met me at the door and kissed me. "How's my conquering hero?"

I forced a smile. "Conquered."

"Did something go wrong?"

I leaned back and looked into her face. "We'll talk about it later." We kissed again. "Something smells good."

"It's my new perfume. Dolce&Gabbana's 'The One.' "

"I meant the food. But you smell good too."

"Thanks," she said. "I got some of that salami you like from Giuseppe's and, my big surprise, I made my first tiramisu."

"*Fantastico*," I said with a bad Italian accent. "I brought this." I lifted the bottle of wine.

She studied the label. 2002 Ruffino Chianti. "Good choice. Everything's ready. Let's eat."

We sat down at her small table. I uncorked the wine and filled her glass halfway. She swished the wine around, then sniffed the burgundy liquid.

"That's nice. Fruity."

I sipped the wine and was about to take a much-needed longer drink when Ashley said, "Wait. We should toast."

I stopped the glass on the way to my lips. "What would you like to toast?"

"Your career, of course. No, the future." She raised her glass. "To the future."

"The future," I repeated dully. I nearly drained my glass.

"So tell me about this tough day."

"It can wait," I said.

"No, then it will just hang over our evening like a cloud. Tell me now, then we'll move on to having fun."

I finished my drink, set down my glass and took a deep breath. "All right. Here it goes. I'm leaving Jacobson."

She blinked in disbelief. "What?"

"I've taken a job with another firm. A bigger one."

Her expression fell. "You're leaving your family's business? You're going to own that place one day."

"I took a job in Chicago. It's an agency called Leo Burnett. It's one of the biggest firms in America. There's lots of potential. It's a chance to—" I borrowed Simon's words—"spread my wings."

She looked stunned. "Chicago? What's wrong with spreading your wings in Colorado?"

"Colorado," I said, wading through my excuses. "It's just too small of a market. There's not enough sky." I filled my glass with more wine. "This is a great opportunity."

Ashley just stared at me. Then tears began welling up in her eyes. "You can't do this."

I breathed out slowly. "It's a done deal. I've already accepted the job and resigned from Jacobson."

"Then unresign."

"You can't unresign."

"Of course you can. This isn't some global conglomerate, it's your family. You can do whatever you want!" Her lips tightened in anger. "You couldn't have talked to me about this first?"

I didn't know how to answer her. "I had to . . ."

"Had to? You had to what? Throw everything away? We're here celebrating your first big campaign, your big break at your family's firm, and now you're leaving? Did your first success just go to your head?"

I didn't answer. I couldn't answer.

She took a drink of wine, then put her hand over her eyes. "I can't believe this. Tell me you're kidding before I melt down."

"I'm sorry. Everything just happened so fast."

"And how do I fit into this?"

"You'll come with me."

She looked at me incredulously. "I'm supposed to just pull up my roots? What about *my* career? Things are just starting to take off for me."

"I know," I said. "It's not fair. But there will be bigger opportunities in Chicago. Chicago has some of the biggest modeling agencies in the country."

"Like I'll have a chance breaking into one of those?"

"Why wouldn't you?"

"Because big-time models spend their lives becoming big-time models." She shook her head. "I can't believe this."

"Ashley, just have a little faith. It's going to be great. It's a chance for us to strike out on our own."

Tears began to fall down her face. She wiped her eyes and said, "With or without you, I'm not leaving Denver."

Her words stunned me. "What?"

"I'm not leaving. Everything, everyone I love is here."

"Except me," I said.

"That's your choice, not mine. If you love me, you'll stay."

I felt like my heart was going to stop. "You really would leave me?"

"Don't turn this around. You're the one leaving. If your ambition is more important than me . . ." She wiped her eyes with her napkin, then stood. "I can't believe you're doing this. I can't believe it."

"I had to." I stood and walked up to her.

"No you didn't." She wiped her eyes again. "When are you leaving?"

"Tomorrow around one."

She let out a small gasp. "You tell me the day before?"

"Ashley . . ."

"I think you better go now."

"I know this isn't fair. Why don't we wait a few months, I'll get things settled in Chicago, then you can come out and . . ."

She looked at me quizzically. "And what?"

"Get married. Start our family."

She looked at me with surprise. "I never said I wanted to marry you."

"What?"

"It's not just you. I don't want to be contractually tied down to someone."

"But you said you love me."

"I do love you. But I don't know if you're the one I want to spend the rest of my life with."

I stared at her speechlessly.

"Joseph, we're happy the way we are. Why would you want to get married?"

"Because I love you," I said.

"If you love me, you'll stay in Denver."

Tears began to fill my eyes. "I'm sorry."

She took a deep breath before saying "Then so am I." She covered her eyes with one hand, then said, "I think you had better go."

"Ash . . ." I leaned forward to touch her, but she backed away. I exhaled slowly. "Okay," I said.

She didn't say another word to me as I left her apartment. On the drive home I thought my heart would break.

When I left the agency, I thought my world had fallen apart. But now it was completely shattered. When I pulled into my driveway, I couldn't stop crying.

# CHAPTER

## Eight

*Today I left for a new city but arrived in a new world.*

✦ Joseph Jacobson's Diary ✦

I guess some stupidly optimistic part of me hoped that Ashley would show up at my apartment before I left, but as the taxi pulled away from my curb, there was no sign of her. No romantic cavalry riding in to save the day. There was nothing to save.

I think my heart felt heavier than my bags, which is saying something since I ended up having to pay a fee for overweight luggage. Just like that, my Ashley was gone. What was worse is that she wasn't even mine. She never had been. I didn't blame her for being upset. I knew I had pulled the rug out from under her, but I guess I'd expected her to fight harder to keep us. To keep me.

Aside from Ashley, I left Colorado without saying goodbye to anyone. I might as well have just vanished.

The landing at O'Hare was pretty rough, which seemed appropriate. I waited nearly an hour at the carousel for my luggage, then waited again in line for a cab. The taxi driver, a stocky, dark-featured man with puffy eyes and an accent I didn't recognize, put my bags in the trunk. He slammed the trunk and we both climbed inside the car.

"Where you going, pal?" the driver asked.

"Jefferson Park area," I said, repeating what the landlady had told me to say.

"You have an address?"

"Yes." I handed him the slip of paper I'd written the apartment's address on.

He examined my note, then said, "No problem." He pulled away from the curb.

Twenty minutes later the taxi stopped in a sedate neighborhood on a corner of Lawrence Avenue near an ugly white apartment building. Rusted, gray satellite dishes stuck out from its side, and the bricks under the windows were painted baby blue. The driver lifted my bags from the trunk, dropping them heavily on the sidewalk.

"How much do I owe you?" I asked.

"Twenty-two dollars," he said.

I handed the man two twenties. "Could I have sixteen dollars back please?"

"*Skapiec,*" he mumbled. He took the money from me, then drew the bills from his wallet and handed them to me.

I looked at the names listed on the outside mailbox. Five of the six were Polish. The lobby was dirty, with heavily stained carpet, and it smelled of cabbage. The pale green plaster walls were well marked and chipped, almost as worn as the wood banister that ran up the stairs.

I could hear U2 playing from one of the apartments. "With or Without You." Ashley loved U2. She loved Bono. She would have followed Bono to Chicago.

It took two trips to lug my bags up the narrow flight of stairs to the second floor. I had called my new landlady from a payphone in the Denver airport to make sure everything was ready. She was a gruff-sounding woman. She was unable to meet me but had left my apartment key with a neighbor. "He'll be home," she said. "Two-zero-seven is always home."

I knocked on the door to apartment 207. No one answered. *What if he wasn't home?* I waited a couple minutes then knocked again. To my relief, I heard footsteps and a muffled voice said, *"Chwileczke, chwileczke."* A moment later the door opened a few inches, stopped by a chain. I could see a slice of face, an elderly man with gray-white hair.

"What you want?" he said with a thick accent.

"Mrs. Walszak told me you'd have the key to my apartment."

*"Co?"*

He looked confused, so I spoke more slowly. "Mrs. Walszak told me you would have the key to my apartment."

"Da key?"

"Yes. The key."

"What your name?"

"Joseph Jacobson."

"Wait." The door shut again. I expected to hear the door unlock, but instead there was the sound of the footsteps, which quickly dissipated. I stood there another few minutes wondering if the man would be coming back or if I should knock again. Then I heard a toilet flush and the footsteps again, followed by the slide of the chain and a deadbolt. The door opened. The man looked at me with an annoyed expression, then held out a key in his thick hand. "Here is da key. I tell Mrs. Walszak."

"Thank you," I said. "I'm Joseph."

"Balwan," he said. "Don't make much noise." He shut the door in my face.

I exhaled. "Nice to meet you too, neighbor." I turned around and unlocked my door, then grabbed my bags and dragged them inside.

The apartment was as plain as a boxcar—a small flat with an electric range and a miniature fridge that was circular on top like an antique. The walls were painted eggshell white but marred with nail holes and tape residue.

I turned on the light, which was just an exposed bulb. The room smelled of cabbage and mold.

It was cold enough to see my breath. "Welcome home," I said facetiously. There was an iron radiator in the corner of the room. I walked over to it and turned a knob. It began to creak.

I checked out the bathroom. It had an old porcelain sink on metal legs, a toilet and a shower bath with a brittle, semi-transparent plastic shower curtain imprinted with blue and green turtles wearing top hats.

I walked over to the bedroom and sat on the bed. The sheets were gray from age and the mattress sagged a little in the middle.

The landlady had told me that the apartment was furnished, which, in this case, meant a small round kitchen table with two wooden chairs, a cigarette-burned swaybacked sofa likely abandoned by a former tenant during the sixties, the bed and a small chest of drawers.

The apartment was cheap by Chicago standards but would still cost me nearly twelve hundred a month—four hundred more than my apartment in Denver. I had some money in the bank, around ten thousand, and the three thousand Rupert had given me, but that was all there was between me and the curb. I didn't know what the Leo Burnett agency paid.

I unloaded my suitcases into the dresser. I had forgotten my iron, so I lay my suit coat on the bed and hand pressed out the wrinkles for my first day at work in the morning.

I walked over to the window and raised the blind. In spite of the cold, I opened the window and let in some fresh air. I stuck my head out to survey my new surroundings. The street was quiet. About two blocks from my apartment was a grocery store, and I suddenly remembered that I hadn't eaten anything that day. I put on my coat and walked out, locking the door behind me.

The market was on the corner of Lawrence and Austin, and on my way there I passed a hair salon, two bakeries (one Polish, one Sicilian), a dental office and a real estate office.

## J&L European Deli
### Wlasny Wyrob Wedlin

I guessed that the words under the market's name were Polish, and my hypothesis was confirmed as I walked inside and was greeted by the pungent smell of meats and sausages and loud talking in what I assumed must be the Polish language.

With the exception of Coca-Cola, everything inside was Polish, including the periodicals on the magazine stands. The shelves were stacked with rows of foods with strange names. I bought some basic staples and a few housewares— they didn't have many—some paper towels, dishwashing soap, a pan, measuring cups and spoons, a plastic drinking cup, a plastic bowl, a plate, and two sets of utensils. I wasn't planning on entertaining anyone; I just needed an extra set while the other was waiting to be washed.

A young man walked out from behind the deli counter and met me at the cash register. He spoke perfect English. I paid for my purchases, then walked back home.

Once I was home, I poured myself a bowl of granola, cut a banana into it, then added milk. When I had finished eating, I went into my room and pulled down the sheets, then took off my clothes. I shut off the light and lay down on the bed.

My heart ached. I had too much on my mind to sleep, mostly things I didn't want to think about. How was it that you could be speeding through life on a set course, then, in just one day, have the tracks changed beneath you?

As I lay there in my strange surroundings, my despair turned to anger. I had been *banished*. Banished from Denver.

*Who gets banished from Denver?* Other questions loomed omi-
nously, like powder kegs of anxiety. What would my father
and mother do when they found out I had left?

What weighed heaviest on my heart was how wrong I'd
been about Ashley. I was just months away from asking her
to marry me. I was ready to make the biggest commitment of
my life, and she wasn't even considering it. I suppose I should
have been glad to find this out now, but it didn't do much to
take away the pain.

After tossing and turning for what seemed like hours, I
got back out of bed and set up my computer on the kitchen
table. Fortunately, the apartment had wireless Internet. I had
to find my notes from the landlady, because the apartment's
password had like six consonants and one vowel. I was glad I
didn't have to learn Polish.

On a whim, I went to Facebook and looked up Ashley's
page. She'd already changed her relationship status to "single." There were a couple dozen posts with condolences
from her girlfriends and co-models, mostly bashing me.
She had graciously accepted their comments with contrived
humility and eager victimhood. In one comment, she had
magnanimously defended me with "He has his good points."
Wow. *How could I have been so wrong about her?*

With everything on my mind, I felt restless. I put my coat
on and went back outside to the dark street. I wasn't sure
whether or not it was a safe neighborhood, but it looked
liked one. At least it was quiet.

I walked toward the market with my hands in my

pockets, past the façades of apartments and small busi-
nesses hung with CLOSED signs. West of the market I spotted a neon sign glowing OPEN. I crossed the street toward
it. Mr. G's Diner. I pushed the door open and walked
inside.

# CHAPTER

## *Nine*

*The great introductions of our lives usually arrive quietly
and untrumpeted, appearing like the piece of paper in
a show's* Playbill *announcing a cast change.*

✦ Joseph Jacobson's Diary ✦

The diner was small, with a half-dozen vinyl-seated booths, two tables and six chairs along the bar, beneath the diner's menu. The place was empty except for a young woman standing behind the counter wiping it down. She looked close to my age, maybe a year or two older.

She was pretty, though in a dressed-down way, as if she were trying to hide it. She had light brown hair that fell to her shoulders, with an errant strand falling over her face. Her eyebrows were slightly darker than her hair, accenting her almond-shaped eyes. She had full lips though she didn't wear lipstick or any other makeup.

She continued wiping the counter, oblivious to my entrance.

"Hi," I said.

Nothing. Then I noticed the white cord under her chin. She was wearing earbuds. I stood there for a moment, then moved in front of her and waved. "Hi," I said.

She jumped back with a small gasp. She pulled out her earbuds. "You scared me."

She had a soft, raspy voice. Her eyes were bright green.

"Sorry," I said. "Could I get a cup of coffee?"

She didn't answer right away, but looked me over with a strange expression. Finally, she said, "Uh, sure. What would you like?"

"Just a decaf. With milk."

"Okay. Give me just a minute. You can sit down, I'll bring it out to you."

"Thank you."

I had the pick of the place. I chose a table near the shuttered front window. She walked over to the diner's front door and flipped a switch on the sign, locked the door, then returned to the counter. A couple minutes later she brought out my coffee with a cream-cheese Danish.

"I didn't order the—"

"I know," she said. "I'm not charging you for it. It's the end of the night so I was about to throw it out anyway. You don't have to eat it if you don't want to."

"No, it looks good. Thank you."

"You're welcome." She walked back to the counter and set back to work. I slowly sipped my coffee, examining my surroundings. The place was clean, its sky blue walls decorated with simply framed portraits, some black and white photographs, some sketches or drawings. I recognized some of the faces, like Ronald Reagan, John Belushi, Raquel Welch, Walt Disney and Robin Williams. But there were more I didn't recognize. I tried to figure out what they had in common, but the connection eluded me.

The diner was quiet. There was no music playing, no noise at all except the sound of the woman putting things away behind the counter.

I asked, "Are you always this slow?"

She gave me a strange look.

"I mean, the shop. Not you."

"No. We're closed."

"What time do you close?"

"Midnight."

I looked down at my watch. It was eleven-forty. "It's still twenty to," I said.

"It's twenty to one," she replied.

I looked back down at my watch. I'd forgotten to change it with the time change. "Sorry. I'm on the wrong time zone."

She didn't say anything.

"So it was already midnight when I came in," I said.

"I forgot to lock the door."

"Thanks for letting me in."

"It's okay."

I heard the ring of a cash drawer. "Would you mind paying now so I can close out the till?"

"Not at all." I pulled out my wallet. "How much do I owe you?"

"Five. Two for the coffee. Three for the pastry."

"But . . ."

"I'm just kidding. Two dollars."

I walked over to the counter and handed her a five anyway. "Keep the change."

She took the money. "A three-dollar tip for a two-dollar coffee?"

"That's for staying open late."

"Thanks. You said you're on a different time zone?"

"I just flew in."

"Is this your first time at Mr. G's?"

I nodded. "Yes. I just moved here."

"How long ago?"

"About eight hours."

"You are fresh. Where did you come from?"

"The west. Denver."

"I'm from Utah."

"Utah," I said. "I've been to Salt Lake City at least a dozen times. We had a client there. Beautiful city."

"I'm not from Salt Lake," she said. "I'm from southern Utah."

"I've been there too. The St. George area?"

"Not too far from there."

"There's some beautiful scenery in that area, Zion National Park, Bryce Canyon, the Grand Canyon."

"Yes there is," she said. "And lots of tourists."

"What brought you to Chicago?" I asked.

"I needed a change of scenery. How about you? Work?"

"Yes." Then I added sardonically, ". . . And family." I gestured to the portraits. "So, I've been trying to figure out what all these people on the walls have in common."

"They're all famous people from Chicago."

"Oh," I said. "That makes sense. But I can't figure out who some of them are." I pointed to a picture of a middle-aged man with short auburn hair and wire-rimmed glasses.

"That's Robert Zemeckis. He's a film director."

"Right," I said. "He made *Back to the Future.*"

She shrugged. "I'll take your word for it."

"You've never seen *Back to the Future?*"

She shook her head. "I've never heard of it."

"With Christopher Lloyd and Michael J. Fox?"

She shook her head again.

I looked at her quizzically. "How could you not have heard of *Back to the Future?*"

"I'm not much into movies," she said.

"All right," I said, pointing to another picture. "Who's that guy?"

"Edgar Rice Burroughs. He wrote *Tarzan.*"

"Do you know everyone in here?"

"Everyone except you."

"I'm Joseph."

"Nice to meet you, Joseph. I'm April."

I took another sip of my coffee. "April. Were you born in April?"

"No, but my sister was." She paused. "Her name is June."

I grinned. "And you were born in June?"

"No, my brother August was. I was born in August."

I laughed. "You're making this up."

"Nope. It's the honest truth."

"April, June and August. Any other months?"

"I also have a sister named January."

"It's a good thing your family isn't as big as mine."

She gave me an amused look. "And why is that?"

"You'd run out of months," I said. "There are thirteen of us."

She didn't overreact to the number like most people did. "That's a big family," she said.

"Actually, it's four families. My father's been married four times."

"Where do you fall in the lineup?"

"Last wife, second-to-the-last kid. I have a younger brother."

"You're almost the baby," she said. She glanced over my shoulder. "Your coffee's getting cold. Hand me your cup and I'll freshen it for you."

"You don't have to do that," I said. "I'm sorry, I've kept you late enough."

She pulled a strand of hair back from her face. Her eyes looked tired but were still soft and kind. For a moment I just stared at her. "That's okay," she said. "I still need to record the receipts. Get your coffee."

I retrieved my cup. She dumped out the remaining coffee and filled it again, topping it off with milk. "There you are. And no hurry, I've still got at least twenty minutes of things to do to close up."

"Thank you. I promise I won't bother you again."

"You're no bother. It's nice to have company."

I carried my cup back to my table while April disappeared through a back door. I continued looking around the room at the portraits, quizzing myself until my coffee was gone. I returned my cup to the counter. "April?"

She walked out from the back. "Finished?"

"Yes. I'd just let myself out, but I didn't want to leave the door unlocked." I smiled wryly. "You never know who might wander in."

She smiled back. "No, you never know. I'll let you out."

I followed her to the door. She unlocked it, then put out her hand. "It was nice meeting you, Joseph. I hope you come back sometime."

"It was my pleasure. Thank you for the . . ." I was going to say coffee, instead I said, ". . . kindness."

*"Kindness,"* she echoed. For a moment neither of us moved. She looked at me intently, then said softly, "Do you know you have sad eyes?"

Her question surprised me. "No. But it's kind of a hard time." I turned to go. "Thank you. Good night."

I had only taken a step when she said, "Joseph."

I turned back.

"Besides Robert Zemeckis, do you know anyone in Chicago?"

I shook my head. "Not a soul."

"Maybe I could show you around sometime?"

Her offer surprised me. "I'd like that. When?"

"What's your schedule like?"

"I'm not sure—I'm just starting a new job, but it's probably the usual nine to five. How about you?"

"I work every day, but I have the weekends off. How about this Saturday?"

"Saturday would be good."

"Do you want the day tour of Chicago or the nickel tour?"

"What's the difference?"

She cocked her head. "About three hours."

"I've got the whole day."

"Then it's the day tour. How about we meet here at nine. I'll make you breakfast."

"That sounds good. Nine it is. I'll look forward to it."

"Me too. Good night, Joseph."

"Good night."

Buttoning my coat, I stepped out onto the sidewalk. April locked the door behind me. In the time I'd been inside the diner the temperature had noticeably dropped and I walked briskly back to my apartment. Still, as cold as it was, I hardly noticed it. I guess I was pleasantly distracted.

Unfortunately, reality was still waiting for me back at my apartment and I tossed in bed most of the night. Too many unknowns. Too much to wonder. Too much to fear.

I wondered if my father would take my disappearance as betrayal or ingratitude. And I wondered if Ben's guilt would get the better of him and if he'd tell my parents. As lonely and anxious as I was, I hoped he wouldn't. My father would be furious with Ben, and considering how ruthless he'd been with my brothers of late, there was no telling what he might say or do to them. After all that had happened lately, this might not just destroy the agency, but the family as well. I didn't want that for my father or them.

The best thing—the only thing—would be for the brothers to have a change of heart and bring me back home. As I looked up into the darkness, I wondered if that was even possible.

✦

After a mostly restless night, I woke to the annoying beep of my travel alarm clock. The apartment's radiator was more bark than bite, and in spite of its incessant groaning and clanking, my apartment was freezing. I dragged myself out of bed and stepped barefoot onto the cold hardwood floor.

I went into the bathroom and turned on the shower. The showerhead emitted a narrow, unsatisfying stream of tepid water.

I remembered my high school football coach razzing me with "Jacobson, you're so skinny, you have to run around in the shower to get wet." That was almost true in this shower, though my weight had nothing to do with it.

I had forgotten to buy soap, so I stepped out of the shower, only then realizing that I had also forgotten to pack a towel. I walked to the kitchen dripping wet and grabbed the dish-washing soap and paper towels. I washed my hair with the soap, which worked surprisingly well, then wiped myself dry with paper towels.

The Leo Burnett agency was located on Wacker Drive in Chicago's main business district, an area nicknamed the "Loop." It was also just southwest from Michigan Avenue and what Chicagoans call the Magnificent Mile, an upscale section of the city containing department stores, restaurants and hotels.

When I had called for information on the apartment, Mrs. Walszak had given me directions to the Leo Burnett office. I was told to walk to the Jefferson Park station and take the Blue Line of the 'L,' the elevated train, to the Clark/Lake station, which would let me off just a half block from the Leo Burnett building.

It took me less time to get to work than I had planned, so I got a coffee in the building's lobby.

I felt like a kid on the first day of school in a new town. I hoped they played nice.

# C H A P T E R

*Ten*

*Last night I had a peculiar but hopeful dream. I was in a photo studio. Everything was white and lit so brightly it was difficult to see. Suddenly there was a man wearing an orange suit, orange sneakers and an orange shirt and bow tie. He was leaning against a black cane.*
*"Welcome to the first day of your new life," he said,*
*flipping his cane. "This is where we play hardball."*
*"Do you think I'll make it?" I asked.*
*He looked at me with a wry grin then said,*
*"You can bank on it."*

✳ Joseph Jacobson's Diary ✳

Chicago is home to some of the greatest advertising agencies and admen of all time—pioneers in marketing like Albert Lasker, Fairfax Cone and the great copywriter Claude C. Hopkins.

These names may mean nothing to you, but they should. These Chicago men defined advertising before the world even knew what it was. They have influenced your life far more than you know, and likely want to believe. For instance, if you drink orange juice, you've been affected by Lasker, because before he sold us packaged orange juice, people only *ate* oranges.

These legends of marketing have made household names of brands like Goodyear, Van de Kamp's, Quaker Oats, Marlboro and Palmolive. The fact that many of the campaigns that defined these brands were designed nearly a century ago makes it even more astounding.

Leo Burnett, the founder of the agency that had hired me, was also one of the pioneers of the field, and the agency that bears his name is legendary. Burnett, who started his agency in the midst of the Great Depression, understood how to reach people through imagery. He gave us cultural icons that survive today: Tony the Tiger, the Pillsbury Doughboy, Charlie Tuna, the Jolly Green Giant and the Marlboro Man. For a young adman, I was walking hallowed halls where the giants of the industry had walked.

I was stopped near the elevator by a security guard who walked me to the first elevator and rode it with me to the twenty-first floor. "This is your stop," she said.

The reception area was contemporary and hip: frosted green glass panels lined the wall, behind a white reception counter nearly 50 feet long seating nine or ten employees. The ceiling was open, exposing ductwork and lighting fixtures, all of which were painted black. On the far end of the counter, hanging from the ceiling, was a pair of eyeglasses 12 feet long, as iconic to Leo Burnett as the cigar was to Churchill.

At the reception desk, a young Asian woman with a telephone headset and orange hair even shorter than mine, looked up to greet me. "May I help you?"

"I'm here to see Peter Potts."

"May I ask your name?"

"Joseph Jacobson."

"Thank you, Mr. Jacobson." She pressed a button on her phone. A moment later she said to me, "Someone will be right with you. Have a seat, please."

A few minutes later a young woman walked around the corner from the far end of the reception area. She was probably a couple years older than me, with long blond hair. She smiled at me as she approached. "Mr. Jacobson?"

"Yes, ma'am," I said, standing.

"I'm Kim. Mr. Potts has been delayed a few minutes. He's asked me to show you upstairs."

The elevator's ceiling was paneled in colorful stained glass set in a pattern that looked like a Frank Lloyd Wright sketch. We got out on the twenty-seventh floor.

"This building is the Leo Burnett Worldwide headquarters. We have sixteen floors and more than seventeen hundred employees. Twenty-seven is one of our creative floors."

Kim led me into a large open office space, a jungle of cubicles, each individually decorated to show its tenant's creativity and personality—the Monopoly guy, a jungle, a collector of superhero figurines, and a *Wizard of Oz* fan. One cubicle was simply painted with jail bars.

"Here's your desk," Kim said, leading me to a plain cubicle. "I'll call you when Mr. Potts arrives."

"Thank you," I said.

After she'd gone, I looked over my small, austere cubicle. I sat down and sighed. Back in Denver I had had a private office. *One of many changes*, I thought.

Painted in rainbow colors on the wall across from me was:

> **We are**
> **eternal**
> **students of**
> **human**
> **behavior**

"You're the new guy," a thin, tinny voice said behind me. I turned around to see a man leaning against my cubicle. He was tall and blond, with a slight underbite. I pegged him at a year or two younger than me. He wore John Lennonish, wire-rimmed glasses.

"I'm Len," he said. "Abbreviated Leonard. Senior writer. Call me Len."

"Joseph," I said.

"No," he said. "It's Len."

"No, I'm Joseph."

"Right," he said. "Joe."

I'd never really liked being called Joe, and outside of my father, no one did. "Joseph," I repeated. "Or J.J."

"J.J. What are you, a rapper?" He pulled a chair from an empty desk across from mine and sat down, looking me over.

"Nice suit," he said.

"Thanks."

"No one wears suits here. Not in this century."

"Noted."

"Where are you from, J.J.?"

"Denver."

"Go Broncos. I still miss Elway. What agency?"

"A regional firm. Jacobson Advertising."

"Never heard of it," he said. "So this is your first time adrift in the big sea." He leaned in closer. "Let me tell you how we sail in the Windy City. If you want to survive, put in your time, keep sharp and stay below the radar. Potts is a beast. Creative, good at his job, but a beast. Have you met him?"

"Not yet."

"Be warned, he believes it necessary to sacrifice a writer from time to time *pour l'encouragement des autres.*"

I tilted my head. ". . . To encourage the others?"

*"Exactemente, mon ami,"* Leonard replied. "You speak French?"

"Just what I learned in high school," I said. I looked at him as he wiped his forehead with his sleeve. "What if you want to do more than just survive?"

Leonard shook his head. "Ambitious. Good for you. Get over it. The rest of the writers will hate you and they'll offer you up to Potts as a sacrificial lamb."

"I'll be careful," I said.

"Be careful or be gone," Leonard said. He grinned. "Not a bad line. I'm going to hang on to that." Then his eyes flashed and he abruptly stood and walked away. Actually, he fled. I turned back to see a man walking from the main hallway toward my cubicle. He was tall, 6 feet 3 or so, muscular and bald. He wore a black silk T-shirt beneath a silver jacket. His gaze was on me.

"Are you Jacobson?"

"Yes, sir."

"Come with me."

I guessed he was Potts. "Yes, sir," I said. I stood and followed him. He walked to a corner office at the end of a long row of cubicles. The walls of his office were decorated with framed print ads. He sat down behind a large glass desk, eyeing me grimly. "Shut the door."

"Yes, sir." I pulled the door shut.

"You go by Joe or Joseph?"

"Joseph or J.J., sir."

"Sit down, Joseph."

I sat.

"Let's be clear on something. You're here by my approval but not my choice. Timothy Ishmael convinced me that we had to have you. But that only got you through my door and that door swings both ways. If I don't like what I see, you'll see the backside of that door. Do you understand?"

"Yes, sir."

"I don't know what lame advice Leonard was imparting, but do yourself a favor and disregard it. The man's on vocational life support."

"Yes, sir. Thank you, sir."

"What's with all the, 'yes, sirs'? This isn't the military."

"Sorry. My father's a veteran. It's habit."

A barely distinguishable smile crossed his lips. "I see. Mine too. What branch?"

"Navy. He served in Vietnam as a pilot. He was in the Gulf."

There was a single knock on the office door. Then the door opened and a woman minced into the room with obvious familiarity. Potts lit up when he saw her. "Do you have time for lunch?" she asked.

The woman was stunningly beautiful, tall, even without the 3-inch heels she wore. She had auburn hair that fell to her shoulders. She realized they weren't alone. "Who is this?"

"New guy," Potts said dismissively.

"Hello, new guy," she said.

"Hi," I said.

She looked back at Potts. "Does new guy have a name?"

"Joseph," he said. "Or T.J."

"J.J.," I said. "Shall I go?"

"Get out of here," he said. "Have Kim show you around. We've got a staff meeting at one. Be there."

I stood. "Okay. Thank you. And nice to meet you," I said to the woman.

She looked me over and smiled. "Ditto."

I walked out of the office, stopping at Kim's desk which was right outside Pott's office. She was typing at her computer and glanced up at me. "May I help you?"

"Mr. Potts told me to ask you to show me around."

"Just let me finish this email . . ." She typed a half-minute more, then stood. "Okay, let's take the tour."

Kim gave me a tour of the three floors most relevant to the copywriters, including the employee break room, three conference rooms and the employee cafeteria.

Near the elevators, she pointed to a large room. "This is the energy room. There's one on each of the creative floors. It's where you can go to chill and let your mind explore."

Behind a glass partition was a large room with a foosball table, soda machine, refrigerator, popcorn kettle and cart, and stools and chairs. The outer walls were all glass, looking out over the tops of neighboring skyscrapers.

She concluded my tour at the supply closet, where she outfitted me with office essentials, then helped me carry everything back to my desk. We passed Leonard on the way back to my cubicle, but he didn't even acknowledge me. Kim was pleasant and likable—almost the opposite of her boss.

"How long have you been here?" I asked.

"Five years this coming June."

"Then you've been here awhile. What's your title?"

"I'm Mr. Potts's personal assistant."

"What is that like?"

Her brow furrowed. "Every day's an adventure."

We set all the supplies on my desk. "There you are," Kim said. "Welcome to the agency."

"Thank you."

As she was leaving me, I said, "Mr. Potts said there's a staff meeting at one. Where will that be?"

"His office. Call if you need anything. Just press four-two-five."

"Four, two, five," I repeated. "What should I do until then?"

She cocked her head. "Look busy."

# CHAPTER

## *Eleven*

*Today another dream was realized—just not the one I hoped for most.*

✦ Joseph Jacobson's Diary ✦

By noon almost everyone on the floor had left for lunch. I walked down to the cafeteria and got myself a chicken Caesar salad, which I ate alone, then went back to my cubicle.

At five minutes to one I grabbed a yellow pad and pen and walked over to Potts's office. In addition to Kim, there were six other people gathered near his door. The group was evenly divided between men and women. I was the only one in a suit.

One of the men, short, thin, and narrow-hipped, with red hair and glasses, put out his hand. "I'm Timothy Ishmael. Welcome to Burnett."

"You're the one who got me the job," I said.

Timothy nodded. "I'm the team manager. I met your brother, Simon, three years ago on a joint project for Sears. He's a good man."

I nodded agreeably though I was miles away from feeling it.

"He really hated to see you go," he said.

"I'm sure he did," I said, trying not to sound sarcastic.

He turned to the others. "This is Sade, Chloe and Kate."

All of them smiled and said hello.

"And you've met Len . . ."

"Unfortunately," Sade said.

"Watch it," Leonard said.

An Asian man standing nearing the door said, "I'm Parker."

"Hi." I pointed at each of them. "Timothy, Sade, Chloe, Kate, Parker and Len."

"That's the team," Timothy said.

Just then Potts's voice came over Kim's phone. "Send them in."

"Yes, sir," Kim said. She nodded at Timothy, who raised his eyebrows.

We walked in single file. A mix of chairs were pulled up around Potts's desk in a tight half-circle. I thought Potts looked even crankier than he had earlier. I wondered if he ever smiled.

"You all meet Jacobson?" he asked after we had sat.

"Yes," Timothy said.

"Good, then we'll dispense with the introductions. I'm not happy, people."

*No surprise there*, I thought.

"I spent an agonizing morning with Cecilia Banks listening to her rant about why our campaign concept for BankOne could be the definition of 'phoning it in.' We have until tomorrow noon to come up with something that blows their minds or, and I quote, 'they'll find someone else who will.' "

"What specifically did they *not like* about our concept?" Timothy asked.

"By 'not like' do you mean 'thoroughly detest'?" Potts replied. "Let me read you the summary." Potts lifted a paper from his desk. "Internal focus test results of the People Caring for People campaign. Here are a few representative comments: Are we advertising a bank or a nursing home? Haven't I already heard that slogan a million times before? Did the chairman's five-year-old son come up with that? Slogan could be the Wikipedia example for the word 'generic.'"

Potts lowered the paper to look at us. "And my personal favorite, 'This is the kind of advertising slogan that makes me want to gouge out my eyes with my BankOne ballpoint pen.'"

Leonard burst out laughing.

Potts glared at him and Leonard immediately stopped.

"I'm glad you find this amusing, Leonard. Because hearing this from our client was anything *but* amusing. We're lucky they didn't walk." He looked over the group coolly. "This is the agency that created the Marlboro Man—I can't believe Edward didn't fire the bunch of us. We have until tomorrow noon to pull a hat trick and show BankOne something worthy of Leo Burnett. And you have until ten-thirty tomorrow morning to present it to me. Don't let me down."

"Did they give you any more specifics?" Timothy asked. "Other than we suck?"

"Original. Memorable. Colloquial. Appeals to the everyman—not just Dom Perignon drinkers."

"We won't let you down," Timothy said.

"You already have. Don't do it again. Wow me. Wow them."

Timothy stood. "On it. Let's go, team."

In spite of Timothy's contrived enthusiasm, gloom had

fallen over the group. When we were out of earshot of Potts's office, Sade said, "Tomorrow morning? Is he serious?"

"As a quadruple bypass," Timothy said. He turned to Parker. "Call Mangia and order sandwiches and Red Bulls. This is going to be an all-nighter."

"Can we have sushi?" Leonard asked.

"No. Everyone has ninety minutes to come up with something. We'll meet in the conference room at three. Kate, have Kim book the room."

She shook her head. "So much for my son's first baseball game," she said.

Leonard turned to me. "Hope you brought your game today, new guy."

I guessed that he had already forgotten my name. "Joseph," I said.

"Right."

I went back to my cubicle and began my creative ritual, scribbling BankOne in ballpoint pen on a yellow notepad. I had never worked on a bank account, though a few years back I had written award-winning copy for a credit union in Thornton. There are few things less titillating than bank advertising, and the name of my award should have been the Less Boring Than the Rest Award.

Then I remembered my dream. *You can bank on it.* I ripped off the page and feverishly began roughing out my concept.

An hour later Parker came by my cubicle. "It's time for our meeting," he said. He sounded grim, more like he was on his way to an execution than a creative meeting. "I'll show you the way."

I grabbed my notepad and followed him to one of the smaller conference rooms—the one decorated with a gigantic box of Froot Loops from our Kelloggs account. Timothy was already inside sitting at the head of the table. He was talking to Kate and shaking his head. Leonard was the last to arrive. He was holding a bag of popcorn and a notepad.

"Shut the door," Timothy said to Leonard.

"Can do, chief." He kicked it shut with his foot.

Timothy took a deep breath. "All right, this is soft-clay phase, no such thing as a dumb idea, just dumb writers. Who wants to go first?"

Everyone looked at each other. Then Kate shrugged. "Don't wait for me, Tim already shot me down."

"Happens," Timothy said. "Sade?"

"Okay. I'm still fleshing it out, so bear with me." She stood. "We're trying to sell credibility, right? So I went back to our original notes and started looking over the trends. BankOne has a larger amount of hospitals as clients than any other major bank. So what if we say, "Four out of five doctors choose BankOne . . .""

No one responded.

"Don't everyone clap at once," she said.

"Comments?" Timothy asked.

Parker shook his head. "No, everyone knows that doctors are horrible with money."

"Overdone," Chloe said.

"Sounds like a joke," Leonard said.

"Take it easy," Timothy said.

Sade sat down. "Fine. Let's see what you've got, Lenny."

Parker stood. "I'll go. I'm with Sade on the credibility. I think she's got the right question just the wrong answer. I say we bring on a celebrity spokesperson, someone people already trust about money, like Suze Orman or Dave Ramsey."

"Are they available?" Timothy asked.

"No idea," Parker said.

"Can we find out before ten-thirty tomorrow morning?"

Parker frowned. "We can try."

"Could work," Sade said.

"They'll never do it," Kate said. "They're not going to tie their names to a specific financial institution. It will taint *their* credibility."

"You never know," Timothy said. "Bob Dole was a pitchman for American Express."

"He also did that Viagra spot," Kate said.

"I think Orman's already linked up with a firm," Sade said.

"Still leaves Ramsey," Timothy said. " Or that Howard guy. The one with the radio show. All right, that's a possibility. Len, what have you got?"

Leonard stood. "All right, people, prepare to lose your socks."

"Just read it," Sade said.

"BankOne. *One heckuva bank.*"

Everyone looked at him dully.

"Are you freaking joking?" Parker said, tossing a crumpled paper at Leonard's face.

Leonard dodged the paper, then said, "Think about it, morons. Behind its simplicity is brilliance."

"Behind its simplicity is a simpleton," Parker said.

"Wow. I think Lenny just called himself brilliant," Chloe said.

"And you called my idea a joke?" Sade said. "Did you even try?"

Leonard turned red. "You people are whack. They wanted something colloquial. That's the way normal people speak."

"What do you know about normal people?" Kate said.

"All right, enough," Timothy said. "Back off." He looked at Leonard. "Is that all you got?"

Leonard sat down. "Yes."

Timothy turned to me. "I know it's your first day, but did you come up with anything?"

"I did," I said, slowly standing. "Bank advertising is tough, because banks aren't sexy. They're not even cool. Personally, I don't want to be sold my bank. I don't even want to think about it. I just want it to be something I *don't* have to think about. Something I can count on. Rock-solid."

"We will rock you . . ." Leonard blurted out.

Everyone ignored him.

"Prudential's already got the Rock of Gibralter," Parker said.

"I'm not saying I want to use a rock," I said. "I'm saying that people just want something solid—especially today. So what do people say when they want to express certainty?"

Everyone just looked at me.

"Bank on it," I said.

Everyone was quiet a moment. Then Timothy said, "I like it."

"Bank on it," Kate said, nodding.

"How will that apply to the customer specifics that our research pulled?" Chloe asked. "Personal touch, solid assets, no hidden fees . . ."

"It fits with all of them," I said. "We can cut right to whatever we're selling with the new tagline. Low fees? At BankOne you can bank on it. Friendly service? You can bank on it."

Sade smiled. "That works."

"I had this other idea too," I said. "We could use a word play on 'BankOne' and 'one bank,' like 'Only one bank offers low fees and high service, BankOne. You can bank on it.' "

Now Timothy was nodding.

I continued. "I liked Parker's idea of using celebrity credibility, but I don't think it needs to be a financial celebrity, just someone who sounds authoritative. I'm thinking we could have Jason Robards voice our tag, the way CNN uses James Earl Jones."

"Robards is a Chicagoan," Chloe said.

"What do you think?" Timothy asked the group.

Everyone was quiet, then Parker said, "I love it. We're commandeering an idiom. It's like the McDonald's 'i'm loving it' campaign."

"It also has graphic capabilities," I said. "We can pull the 'bank on' from the BankOne logo. So, whenever the logo is shown, the tagline is implied."

"Awesome," Kate said.

"Chloe? We still haven't heard your idea."

"I like this one better," she said.

"Len?"

Leonard was still pouting over his rejection. "Where'd you get that idea?" he asked.

"Honestly," I said, "I dreamt it."

"Dream on," Chloe said.

"That's getting paid in your sleep," Parker said.

"All right, Len, assuming that was a 'yes,' we're unanimous. Bank on it. Let's get to work. Chloe, Parker, get me some storyboards and radio scripts. Len and Kate, let's get some preliminary art, in-house usage and style sheets. J.J. and I will put together print. We've got nineteen hours. Go, people." Then he added in Potts's low, gruff voice, "Wow me."

After everyone but Timothy and I had filed out of the room, Timothy said, "Your brother was right."

"About what?" I asked.

"He said you were good under pressure."

"He would know," I said. "The man's a boiler."

# CHAPTER

## *Twelve*

*Time exposes all secrets.*

 Joseph Jacobson's Diary

The team worked until a little after eleven preparing different treatments for the various media. It was a long day, but still about seven hours less than everyone had planned on.

As I walked home from the 'L' station I passed by Mr. G's Diner. The sign was off and the place dark. I pressed my forehead against the glass and cupped my hands around my eyes to look inside. There was a blond woman standing behind the counter. It wasn't April and I think I scared her. I was really hoping that April would be there. I wanted to tell someone about my coup. The truth is, I really wanted to tell my dad. He would have been proud. The thought of him filled me with loneliness. I walked home to my cold apartment and went to bed.

When I arrived at work the next morning, Timothy was already in his office, looking at his computer screen. His door was open and I rapped on his doorframe.

"J.J.," he said, looking over. "Come in. I was just about to call you."

I stepped inside. "What's up?"

"I want you to pitch your idea to Potts with me."

"Be happy to."

"Good. I think they're going to like it." He looked up at his clock, a giant Swatch mounted to the wall. "Let's check on Potts."

He lifted the receiver to his ear. "Kim, would you tell Peter we're ready? Sure." He held nearly a minute before saying, "Thank you." He set the phone back in its cradle. "He's ready." Timothy gathered up the papers we'd prepared the night before, slipping them into a paper file. "Let's 'wow' him."

Kim looked up as we neared Potts's office. "Just go on in."

"Thanks, Kim," Timothy said.

Potts looked angry and tired, like he hadn't slept. I think he was also surprised to see me. As we sat down, he said, "What have you got?"

Timothy said, "You wanted something colloquial, but credible, catchy—"

"Just show me," he said irritably.

"All right." Timothy stood, lifting a sheet. "Only one bank understands all your financial needs. BankOne. Friendly clerks? You can bank on it. Low fees? You can bank on it. Federally insured? Bank on it. BankOne. Bank on it."

Potts sat motionless as he digested the concept, then he held out his hand, gesturing for the pages. "Let me see," he said.

Timothy handed him the layouts and Potts shuffled through them.

"Bank on it," he said. He looked up. "Who came up with this?"

"J.J."

He looked at me without expression. "Okay, let's see if they salute."

We walked out of the office. "I can't read him," I said.

"You could have if he didn't like it," Timothy said.

✦

A little after noon Timothy took me to lunch at a pizza restaurant a half mile from the agency, called Uno.

"You always walk this far for lunch?" I asked.

"No. I usually eat at my desk. But since you're new, and we're almost celebrating, you had to try Uno. This is where the first deep-dish pizza was baked. The guy who invented it was named Ike Sewell. That's his name there," he said, pointing out the window to a street sign. We were at the corner of Ohio and Wabash, but the city had put up a sign that said IKE SEWELL BLVD.

"He never even called it Chicago-style pizza—people called it that after they copied him and took it outside the city. Another testament to the power of a good idea."

After we'd been served, I asked Timothy, "How well do you know my brother?"

"Not too well," he said. "But he obviously made an impression. He was one of the few sane ones on that Sears account." He looked at me. "You flinched when I mentioned his name yesterday. Bad blood?"

"He forced me out of the agency."

Timothy pursed his lips. "That would explain why he was so eager for me to bring you on." He took a bite of his pizza. "I can see why."

"What do you mean?"

"You're a rising star. He's got to feel threatened. Self-preservation and ego are a powerful combination."

I took a drink of my Pepsi. "Unfortunately, my father didn't make the situation any easier. I was his favorite and he didn't care who knew."

"I know that pain from the other side. My younger brother was a high school football star. State quarterback no less. Made my life hell. I was the guy who won the school spelling bee.

"When I told my father I wanted to go into advertising, he told me to get a real job. Today, I've won more than a dozen national awards, my work is seen by millions, and I'm moving billions of dollars of products each year while my quarterback brother does magic shows for kid parties and works as the night manager of a 7-Eleven.

"Not that any of that matters to my father. When we're together at holidays, my father still wants to relive my brother's glory days. It's pathetic, really. He can't even comprehend what I do. All he knows about advertising is what he learned from Darrin Stephens and Larry Tate on *Bewitched*."

"I'm sorry," I said.

"Don't feel sorry for me," he replied. "My life is golden. Stressed, but golden. I feel sorry for my brother. That's quiet desperation for you, knowing your best days are behind you.

Imagine, peaking in high school." He looked down at my plate. "Good stuff, isn't it? Real deep-dish pizza. Nothing better."

I nodded. "We had a Chicago-style pizza place in Denver."

He shook his head. "There's something wrong about that."

We both went back to eating. After a few minutes Timothy said, "I think you're going to do well here. Who knows? Maybe your brother did you a favor."

"Time will tell."

Timothy nodded. "Time is a snitch." He took off his glasses and wiped them with a napkin, then put them back on. "Do you know anyone in Chicago?"

"Other than you and Leonard? No."

"If you need anything, just call. What's your cell number."

"I don't have a phone," I said. "I had to leave it behind. I was going to pick one up yesterday after work, but that didn't happen."

Timothy said, "There's a Verizon store just over on Michigan Avenue. I could write down directions if you want."

"Thanks." I suddenly smiled. "Actually, I do know someone. I met a woman over at a diner near my apartment. She offered to show me around town."

"That sounds promising," he said.

"She was really . . . kind. And beautiful."

"Where do you live?"

"In the Polish area, near Jefferson Park."

"I've been there. Those Polish women. They say that the

Polish women are the most beautiful in Europe, and, even better, they don't know it."

"I don't think she's Polish," I said.

"Well, good luck anyway." Timothy glanced down at his watch. "It's almost one-thirty. The jury should be through deliberating. Let's go check the verdict."

"Nervous?" I asked.

He nodded. "I was born nervous."

A brisk wind blew down Wabash as we made the hike back to the agency.

"Is it always this cold?" I asked.

"Lake effect," Timothy said. "Cuts to the bone."

It took us fifteen minutes to make it back to the Leo Burnett Building. Kate approached us as we stepped out of the elevator. She looked frantic. "Any word?"

"I don't know. We just got back from lunch," Timothy said.

"Where'd you go?" she asked.

"Uno."

She nodded, then turned to me. "Did you love it?"

"What's not to love?" I said.

"You said it." She turned back to Timothy. "Potts has been on the phone since he got back."

"Are you spying on him?" Timothy asked.

"Of course I am."

Timothy leaned forward and whispered to her, "I'll let you know."

We walked back to our desks. I was just settling into my cubicle when my phone rang. "Potts wants to see us," Timothy said.

Timothy tilted his head at Kim and she nodded. Timothy smiled. I took this as a good omen, though seeing Potts's face put doubts back in my mind. He still looked angry. He was leaning back in his chair, glaring at us. We sat down before he asked us to.

"They liked it, didn't they?" Timothy said.

Without smiling, Potts said, "They loved it."

"I knew they would," Timothy said.

"They still need to focus-test," he said.

"Bring it on."

"What were their comments?" I asked.

Potts's gaze focused on Timothy. "They said, 'Next time bring us the good stuff first.'" He looked us over. "Now get out of here. You've got work to do."

We both got up to leave.

"Jacobson, you stay."

I glanced at Timothy. He raised his eyebrows then walked out, shutting the door behind him.

Potts gazed at me for a moment. "Sit."

"Yes, sir." I sat back down.

"So that was your concept."

"Yes, sir."

"You pulled that off pretty fast."

"I come from a small firm. We rarely had the luxury of time."

"As it should be. Some of our people have lost that mentality. Production takes time, but a great idea can come in a millisecond. Where are you from?"

"A small Denver agency. Jacobson."

"Jacobson. That's your last name."

"My father was the founder."

"Family business," he said. "Why did you leave?"

I thought over how much I wanted to tell him. "The pond was too small."

"I understand," he said. "Big fish need room to swim. Did you have any management experience at Jacobson?"

"Some. It was a small firm, but I was over two other copywriters."

"Good. Because I'm putting you over the BankOne creative team. I want you to inspire them. Right after I fire Leonard."

# CHAPTER

## *Thirteen*

*Today was a good day, which gives me hope that there might be others. I don't know if this is the beginning of a new season or the tenuous, tranquil eye of the hurricane.*

✦ Joseph Jacobson's Diary ✦

Friday night I had a dream about April. I don't remember anything about it, just that she was in it. It had to have been something good, though, because for the first time since I left Colorado I woke without dread, which might not be the same thing as waking happy, but under the circumstances, I'd take it.

I checked my watch. Eight o'clock. I showered, using the last of the paper towels to dry myself. Then I dressed, put on my parka and walked down the street to Mr. G's.

The diner was crowded and the line of people waiting to be seated stretched out the door.

Turning sideways, I slid past everyone and walked inside. The place was nearly as frantic as the New York Stock Exchange. There were four waitresses at work, including April, who was standing behind the counter making a cappuccino. She smiled when she saw me. "Good morning. You made it."

"You doubted me?"

"No," she said, then slightly cocked her head. "Maybe."

"You're really busy. Are we still on for today or do you have to work?"

"We're always busy on Saturday mornings, but I'm off. I was just helping out until you came. Have you had breakfast?"

"No."

"Good. I'll get you something." She handed me a menu. "Have a seat at the bar. I'll be right back to get your order."

I took the menu and sat down at the only available seat in the diner. I pondered my choices while April delivered coffees to a table.

"Anything look good?" she asked.

"It all does," I said. "What do you recommend?"

"The feta omelet is my personal favorite. But only if you like feta."

"Sold," I said.

She took my menu and walked back to the kitchen. She returned a moment later. "It will only be a few minutes." She leaned forward on the counter. "So I have a full day planned for us. It's going to take a bit of walking. I hope it's not too cold for you."

"I'm used to cold," I said.

"Of course," she replied. "Denver. But I think it's a different kind of cold here. Denver is pretty dry, isn't it?"

"Yes."

"Here, the dampness just cuts through you. I'm still not used to it. That's why I brought my big coat. And my mittens."

"Me too," I said. "Not my mittens. Just the coat. Do people still wear mittens?"

"I do," she said. "I knit them myself."

"You are a rare woman," I said. She laughed. "So, I'm betting lunch that you really don't know all the people you have hanging on the wall."

"Bring it on," she said.

"Okay, who is that?" I said, pointing to a color photo of a woman.

"Dorothy Hamill. Olympic ice-skater."

I pointed to another woman, a picture in black and white. "And her?"

"Kim Novak. I think she was an actress."

"She was in Hitchcock's *Vertigo* with Jimmy Stewart."

"Hitchcock?" she said.

"Alfred Hitchcock," I said. "You know, the director of *The Birds. Psycho. North by Northwest.*"

She just shrugged. "Never heard of him."

I looked at her quizzically. "Really?"

"I told you I'm not much into movies," she said, taking a step back. "I'll check on our breakfast."

She returned from the kitchen a moment later carrying a tray loaded with plates. She gave me my omelet with a side of hash browns, and a cup of coffee. She set her own meal, a cinnamon roll and a cup of cocoa, on the counter in front of her, then leaned against the counter to eat.

"I'm a sugar freak," she confessed, cutting into the cinnamon roll with a fork. "I'm glad I'm not diabetic. I'd kill myself on those peach gummy candies."

"Those might be worth dying for," I said. "And those grapefruit ones . . ."

"Yes!" she said. "I love those."

"You're standing," I said. I stood. "Come sit."

"No, I'm okay," she said. "I'm just having a roll." A broad smile crossed her face.

"What?" I asked.

"I like that you're a gentleman." She watched me as I took a bite of my omelet. "What do you think?"

"It's good." She looked pleased that I liked it. I took a few more bites. "So what's the plan today?"

"First, we'll go downtown and start our tour at the Sears Tower. Actually, it's not really the Sears Tower anymore, it's the Willis Tower, but everyone still calls it that. I thought we could go to the top so I could show you how the city is laid out. Then we'll go on a walk through Millennium Park. Then over to the Art Institute of Chicago. Then, if we're not too tired, we can walk down by the Navy Pier."

"That's a full day," I said.

"We've got a lot to do. So hurry and eat."

We took the Blue Line to the Clark/Lake station, then walked over to Wacker, passing in front of the Leo Burnett building.

"That's where I work," I said.

April looked up. "That's a very tall building. Does your company use the whole building?"

"We have sixteen floors."

"Wow," she said. "What floor do you work on?"

"The twenty-seventh."

She grimaced. "That's too high."

We walked about eight blocks to the Sears building. The Sears Tower is the tallest building in the Western Hemisphere and the eighth-tallest in the world. From its top floors you can see four states: Illinois, Michigan, Wisconsin and Indiana.

We had been warned by Justyna, one of the cooks at the diner, to expect long lines for the Skydeck but, being winter, there wasn't much of one. I bought our tickets and we got onto the express elevator in less than a half hour, crowded in with about twenty other people.

With the elevator rising two floors a second, it took only sixty-six seconds to get to the Skydeck. A large television screen in the elevator kept us apprised of our skyward progress, informing us, with illustrations, when we'd reached the height of the Sphinx, the Eiffel Tower, and the Empire State Building.

As we stepped out of the elevator, I noticed that April was clearly afraid. No, terrified. As I ventured toward the windows, she remained close to the inside wall. The floor was moderately crowded, and I stayed close enough to the windows to see out, but still near enough to April to talk.

Along the north face of the deck was a series of glass boxes that extended out from the building. "Look," she said. "They built ledges for crazy people."

I saw that if you entered a box, you could walk out over nothing, looking almost 1,400 feet straight down. "That's really cool," I said. "Let's walk on it."

April shook her head, clutching onto the corner of a wall. "No, I hate heights."

"Come on, you know those could hold like five tons."

"I don't care. I hate heights."

"Then why did you bring me up here?"

"I wanted you to see the city."

"You're terrified of heights, but you still came up here for me?"

"Yes." She continued to cling to the wall.

Again, I was taken by her kindness. "Thank you. Would you mind if I walked out on the ledge?"

"No," she said. "I might not look though."

"You don't have to."

"Okay."

I had to wait for a few people in front of me, then I walked out onto the ledge, which, I admit, took a little getting used to. I looked back at April, but a large group had come between us. Instead, I took a picture of my feet with my new phone, then walked back to her.

She looked relieved to see me. "Was it a thrill?"

I grinned. "Yes."

"Good. Can we continue?"

"Of course."

We continued walking around the deck with April staying as close to the inside wall as she could. Finally, I put out my hand. "Come here. That wall's not going to do any good. You can hold on to me."

She swallowed, but still reached out to me. I took her hand in mine. "Now just tell me if we're too close and I'll back away."

"Okay."

We continued our walk around the deck, with me slowly inching closer to the perimeter as we walked. April never told me to stop, though I could tell when she was nervous, as she dug her fingernails into my hand. I never took her closer than ten feet to the window. When we approached the western-facing window, she said, "We live out that way."

"I can see the diner," I said.

"Really?"

"No."

She hit my arm.

One thing I found peculiar was how many men stared at her. I caught at least a half-dozen of them, some with their wives or girlfriends, looking at her longingly. I wondered if she noticed the effect she had on those around her. I doubted it. I thought of what Timothy had said about Polish women and thought it applied to her as well.

When we had walked the entire deck back to the elevators, I asked, "Had enough?"

She nodded quickly. "Yes. Have you?"

I would have denied it if I hadn't. "Yes. Let's go."

She still held my hand while we were in the elevator. Only when we were on the ground floor did she relinquish it.

"I made it," she said.

"Thank you for taking me."

"You're welcome. Before I came to Chicago, I had never been higher than a two-story building."

I looked at her quizzically. "Really?"

She nodded. "I'd never even been in an elevator."

I wasn't sure what to say to that. "That was very brave of you to go all the way up."

"I've done scarier things."

I couldn't help but wonder what they were. We walked outside of the building onto Jackson Boulevard. "Now where?"

"Millennium Park," she said.

"Is that in walking distance?"

"Everywhere is in walking distance," she said. "If you have the time."

I laughed. "Do we have the time?"

"It's only twelve blocks."

Millennium Park ran along Michigan Avenue and we entered along Michigan and Randolph. The park's centerpiece, the Jay Pritzker Pavilion, rose ahead of us with the bandshell's sheets of steel bent like a schooner's sails, reflecting the morning sun.

We got to the edge of the pavilion and looked down.

"There was some controversy when they built this," April said. "The structure was too high for the local ordinances, so they got around it by having it classified as art instead of a building."

"Clever," I said.

"They have concerts here. The acoustics are really good."

"Who have you heard?"

"I've only been here once, but it was the Grant Park Orchestra. They played Rachmaninov's *Symphonic Dances*. It was so beautiful I . . ." She stopped.

"It was so beautiful what?"

"I cried."

"It really made you cry?"

She nodded. "It was like heaven. I kept thinking, I wish I could be that talented, to leave something that beautiful to the world. But I never will. I'm just a waitress."

"I think you have more to offer the world than you think."

"Like what?"

"Beauty."

"Stop it," she said.

"No. I mean it. Real beauty. Soul beauty. I don't think you're like other people."

"What do you mean?"

"I've known you for less than a week and I've seen you demonstrate more acts of genuine kindness than I've seen in some people I've known my entire life."

She didn't say anything.

"I bet you've never intentionally hurt anyone."

"Why would you want to hurt someone?"

"See? That's my point. It doesn't even occur to you to hurt others. Yet you're totally willing to give of yourself to help those around you—like taking the time to show me Chicago. Or going up 103 stories even though you're terrified of heights, because you thought I would want to see it."

"It's not a big deal," she said.

"Yes it is. People just don't do things like that. Especially for people they don't really know."

She looked uncomfortable. "You're embarrassing me. I don't understand why you're saying this."

"Because you called yourself 'just a waitress,' when the truth is, you might be an angel."

She blushed. "If I'm an angel, where's my halo?"

"I think you just leave it at home."

She rolled her eyes. "Shall we go?"

We walked along the length of the pavilion, then cut back near the AT&T Plaza. Ahead of us was a bright silver monument.

"This is my favorite," April said. "It's called *Cloud Gate*. But the people here just call it '*The Bean*.' "

"It looks like a big silver lima bean," I said.

"Or a big drop of mercury," April said.

We walked all the way up to the monument, then underneath, the smooth, voluptuous steel capturing and bending our reflections. Below us, on the other side of the monument, was an ice rink.

"Do you skate?" April asked.

"I can kind of skate."

She took my hand. "Let's do it."

After an hour of ice-skating (and more falls than I care to remember), we ate Chicago dogs with kettle chips at the Park Café, then walked south to the neighboring Art Institute of Chicago.

The museum was hosting a Roy Lichtenstein exhibit featuring 170 works spanning his almost fifty-year career. Every adman worth his carbon knows Lichtenstein's work, as he (like Andy Warhol and his tomato soup can) demonstrated that commercial art can be fine art. April's response to the exhibit was much simpler.

"How fun!"

The sun was falling as we left the exhibit. We walked a mile and a half to the Navy Pier, which, in spite of the season and hour, was still crowded with tourists. The Navy Pier is an amusement park with rides and attractions and its crowning feature is a 150-foot-high Ferris wheel patterned after the first Ferris wheel invented by George Washington Gale Ferris, Jr., for the 1893 Chicago World's Fair.

In keeping with our Chicago-themed day, we snacked on Cracker Jacks and had an ice-cream cone—both Chicago World Fair inventions. (Back then the cones were called cream-filled cornets.)

We walked through the funhouse maze and, at April's coaxing, rode the carousel. Stupidly, I forgot about April's phobia of heights and bought us tickets for the Ferris wheel as well. When I led her toward the amusement, she stopped, staring at the lit wheel in terror. That's when I remembered her fear.

"I'm so sorry," I said. "I forgot. We can just give the tickets to someone."

She stared at the wheel for a moment, then said, "No, I want to do it."

"You don't have to."

"I don't want to let fear run my life."

We shared our gondola with three other people, who seemed to enjoy watching April as much as the ride itself. She clung to me the whole time, which, frankly, I enjoyed, and pretty much kept her face buried in my shoulder anytime we were higher than 20 feet.

As we climbed out of the gondola, our fellow passengers applauded. "Thank you," she said, bowing. "It was nothing. We're going skydiving next."

By 9 P.M. we were both exhausted. Breaking with all things Chicago, we ended up at a Japanese restaurant.

"What a day," I said. "You were running me like a rented racehorse."

She laughed. "I'm glad you like Japanese food."

"Sushi is one of my favorites," I said. "Especially eel."

"I didn't discover sushi until I moved to Chicago. Now I can't get enough. At least when I can afford it, which isn't too often on a waitress's budget." She lifted a gyoza with chopsticks but dropped it. We both laughed.

"I'm not so good with these," she said.

"It takes practice," I said. "Here." I lifted the dumpling to her mouth.

"Thank you," she said, biting into the dumpling. "You know, these are a lot like pierogies."

"I've never had a pierogi," I said.

"Then you haven't lived. That will be our next . . ." She stopped midsentence.

". . . Next date?" I said.

"This isn't a date," she blurted out.

I think her reaction surprised both of us, as she looked a little embarrassed. She added softly, ". . . It's a tour."

I wondered if this was her way of telling me she wasn't interested in a relationship.

"Okay," I said, still reeling a little. "On our next 'tour,' I would love to try a pierogi."

She took a deep breath. "I know this really good Polish restaurant in Logan Square. There are so many good places to eat in Chicago. There are so many different ethnic neighborhoods, you can find anything you want."

"I was here about five years ago with a client. We went to a seafood restaurant called Joe's. Our bill was almost eleven hundred dollars."

"You spent a thousand dollars on one meal?"

"I didn't, my client did. And there were five of us."

"That's still more than two hundred dollars a person. That's almost what I spend on groceries for the month." She looked shocked, or disturbed, as if she were incapable of understanding how someone could spend so much on a meal.

"Some people have money to burn," I said.

"Or eat," she said.

After a moment I said, "You like Chicago, don't you?"

She nodded. "Yes. It's so different from where I'm from."

"What brought you here?"

"Greyhound bus," she said.

I laughed. "I mean why?"

She looked at me for a moment. "My roommate invited me. So how was your first week at your new job?"

I recognized that she was changing the subject, but there was no point in pursuing something she didn't want to talk about.

"My first week was a little surprising."

"Surprising good or surprising bad?"

"Good. I saved a major account and got promoted."

"Hello, Superman," she said. "You're in advertising?"

I nodded. "I'm a copywriter at the Leo Burnett agency— that building we saw this morning. Have you ever heard of it?"

She shook her head. "Not until this morning. Should I have?"

"No, people outside of advertising never know advertising firms' names."

"You would think they would do a better job of advertising themselves."

"They advertise," I said. "Just not to you. That would be wasted money. Unless you're secretly the CEO of a big company."

"No," she said. "Just a waitress."

"Then, the important thing is that you know our clients."

"And who are your clients?"

"McDonald's, BankOne, Nintendo, Hallmark, Coca-Cola, Samsung . . . to name a few."

"Which of those accounts did you save?" she said, sipping her tea.

"BankOne. I came up with their new slogan."

"Can you tell me what it is? Or is it top secret."

"It's top secret, but I think I can trust you with it." I lowered my voice for emphasis. "BankOne. Bank on it." I waited for her reaction. She just looked at me. "What do you think?"

She shrugged. "It sounds good."

"But it doesn't thrill you?"

"Should a bank slogan thrill me?"

"Hopefully."

Her brows fell. "Have you ever been thrilled by a bank slogan?"

"No."

"My point," she said.

"But it thrilled the client."

"That's what matters," she said. "Is that why you came to Chicago? To work at that advertising agency?"

"Sort of . . ." I hesitated briefly, considering whether it was too soon to tell. I decided I didn't care. "But there's more to the story." I looked her in the eyes. "Do you want to know the real story of why I'm here?"

"That depends."

"On what?"

"On whether or not you're an outlaw."

I grinned. "I'm not. At least not yet."

"Good. Because I don't want to end up in court testifying against you." She set down her tea. "So tell me the real story of Joseph Jacobson."

"I was banished from Denver."

"*That* sounds interesting. Go on."

"Remember I told you that my father had thirteen children? Being the youngest, my younger brother and I got more attention than the others, so resentment has been building up with my stepbrothers for years. Last week my stepbrothers found a way to get rid of me. My little brother stole company money. They threatened to send him to prison if I didn't leave the state. So I've been banished to Chicago."

"That's very odd." Her brow furrowed. "I don't understand why your brother stole but you got kicked out. Why didn't they send your brother away?"

"It's because he isn't a threat to them. But they know that I'm close to my little brother, so it was a way to get rid of me."

"So you took the bullet for your brother."

"You could say that."

She thought over my story. "I think it's beautiful that you would sacrifice yourself for your brother, but I hate that your brothers used your love against you. Love should never be used as a weapon."

"Love *is* a weapon," I said.

"No," she said. "It's not. Love is love."

"I'm just saying that people use others' love against them all the time," I said.

She frowned. "I can't argue with that." She finally abandoned her chopsticks and speared a piece of spider roll with her fork. When she'd finished eating it, she said, "That must have been hard on your father. What did he say when you told him you were leaving?"

I slowly shook my head. "I didn't. Part of the deal was that

I wouldn't talk to my parents, so my brothers got to spin the story. I'm sure they'll make it convincing. That's what admen are good at."

"You really were banished." She thought for a moment, then said in a thoughtful tone, "It's a hard thing losing your home and the people you've loved."

She said this as if she truly understood. We went back to eating, and our conversation turned to lighter topics, mostly the experiences of the day: her conquering the Ferris wheel, the number of bruises I'd gotten ice-skating, and the true identity of the woman in the Grant Wood painting *American Gothic*.

"I always assumed it was a picture of a farmer and his wife," I said.

"No," April said, "It's his spinster daughter."

"How did you know that?"

"I study art."

Later in the evening, a Beatles song, "Norwegian Wood," came on over the restaurant's sound system. About halfway through the song, April said, "I like this song. It's pretty."

"I like it too," I replied.

"I wonder who sings it."

"It's the Beatles," I said. "But it wasn't one of their bigger songs."

"Oh," she said. "The Beatles." She took a bite of sushi, then asked, "Are they new?"

I looked at her to see if she was kidding. She just looked back at me.

"No. They've been around awhile."

"I'll have to find some of their music. They're pretty good."

"Yes," I replied. "Some people think so."

It was nearly eleven when April yawned and checked her watch. "Oh my, it's late. We better get on home."

"It's been a nice day," I said. "Thank you for the . . . tour."

"It has been nice," she said. "And it was my pleasure."

I paid the bill, then, with our waiter's help, found the nearest Blue Line station.

As we neared the Irving Park stop, April said, "This is my stop. Yours is two down. After Montrose."

"Should I walk you home?"

"No. It's safe."

As the train approached the station, I asked, "Can I see you again? For another tour?"

She reached into her purse and brought out one of the diner's business cards and scribbled a number on the back of it. "That's my phone number."

The train stopped and the door opened. April hesitated, looking at me, almost as if she wanted a kiss. Then she said, "Call me, please." She touched my arm, then stepped out onto the platform.

I watched her out the window. She just stood there, looking at me with a sweet, sad look. She waved as the train pulled out.

I couldn't figure her out. She had been most adamant that today hadn't been a date, but then she wanted me to ask her out.

The train reached the Jefferson Park station just five minutes later. As I walked home, I realized that even though we'd talked all day, I didn't really know anything about her—except that she seemed to have a peculiar disconnect with popular culture. She knew Rachmaninov and Grant Wood but had never heard of Hitchcock or the Beatles? How could you not know who the Beatles were?

There was more to this woman than met the eye. I was looking forward to finding out what that was.

# CHAPTER

*Fourteen*

*Nothing is so predictable as the dominance of the unpredictable.*

✦ Joseph Jacobson's Diary ✦

The next Monday morning I had been at my desk for less than an hour when Timothy buzzed my cubicle.

"Come see me," he said.

I walked to the office. He was packing the contents of his desk into a box.

"What are you doing?" I asked.

"Did you get the memo?"

"What memo?"

"Leonard's gone."

"That was fast." I leaned against the back wall of his office. "Potts said he was going to fire him. I didn't know if he was serious."

"Potts is always serious," he said.

"Leonard told me he fires people a lot."

"Actually, he's never fired anyone," Timothy said.

"What do you mean?"

"There's too much red tape in firing people. So he demotes them, then transfers them to some remote hellhole, hoping they'll quit."

"Does it work?"

"Usually."

"Is that what he's doing to Leonard?"

"Yes. He'll send him to some satellite office to languish in obscurity. Writers' purgatory."

"How is Leonard taking this?"

"Not well. He's blaming you."

"Why would he blame me?"

"Because Potts told him that you're now in charge of the creative team. So, presumably, it's your decision."

I sat down in one of the chairs. "He said he was going to put me in charge. I have no idea what that means."

"It means you're my boss," Timothy said. "Welcome to your new office."

I looked at him with surprise. "You're kidding me."

"I wish I were."

"I don't want your office," I said. "I thought Potts just wanted me to oversee the Bank On It campaign. I wasn't trying to take your job."

"I know. It's Potts's way of doing business, divide and conquer."

"This doesn't have to divide us, does it?"

"No. It's not like I got a pay cut."

He lifted a large box off of the desk. "There you go. It's all yours."

"Wait," I said. "I'll just tell Potts I don't need an office."

"That's not a good idea," he said. "Potts is a control freak. If you don't take the office, he'll leave it empty before he'd give it back to me. And he'll be angry at you for defying him."

"That makes no sense."

"It does to Potts. To him, life is about gaining power and the burden of protecting it."

"That's just stupid."

"Maybe, but that's how the world turns," he said. He walked to the door carrying a box. "You should know that. That's why you're in Chicago."

That afternoon Potts called me into his office.

"I've scheduled a meeting with the BankOne marketing team for Thursday afternoon. They'd like to brainstorm some direct promotion ideas for increasing clientele."

"What do I need to prepare?"

"Nothing. They just want to talk things out. So how's your new office?"

I resisted saying anything about Timothy. "It has a great view."

A peculiar smile crossed his face. "Speaking of great views, what did you think of Brandi?"

"Brandi?"

"My fiancée. You met her your first day."

"Sorry, I didn't know her name. She's beautiful."

"She's a model. I met her on a photo shoot for Victoria's Secret."

"Burnett has the Victoria's Secret account?"

"Had," he said. "We lost." He looked me over. "What about you? Anyone special?"

"Had," I said. "I also lost the account."

"What did you do to lose it?"

"I came here."

"I had a wife like that. She didn't want to leave Pocatello, Idaho."

I was as surprised to hear that he'd been married as that he was from Pocatello. "You're from Pocatello, Idaho?"

"Someone's gotta be," he said. "The thing is, some people dream in black and white. And some people, like us, dream in Technicolor. You can't change them. All you can do is change the channel."

"I wish it were that easy," I said.

"It is," he said. "The trick is to never fall in love."

# CHAPTER

## *Fifteen*

*I think I'm in love. What a frightening proposition. I don't know
if I speak the language, but I'm pretty sure I don't understand it.*

✦ Joseph Jacobson's Diary ✦

During the next week our team poured out a river of copy to support the new BankOne campaign. Even though I hadn't been there long, I sensed the dynamic had changed. I figured that Leonard must have told everyone that I'd fired him because Parker and the women were acting strangely around me. Unctuous. Fake. I just hoped it would pass.

The week had one highlight. April and I had made dinner plans for the following Wednesday. I told her that I'd meet her at her apartment. I took the Blue Line to her street, then, following the directions she'd texted me, found her apartment.

She opened the door. She was more dressed up than the last time I'd seen her. She wore a light green sweater that accented the green of her eyes. Every time I saw her, I thought she looked more beautiful. "Come in," she said.

Her apartment was small, with a sofa and desk in the front room and no pictures on the wall. Actually, there was one—a picture of Jesus that looked as if it had been cut out of a book or magazine. Across from it was a black and white poster of Kurt Cobain smoking a cigarette. The contrast was strange. April noticed me looking at the poster.

"That's Ruth's," she said. "My roommate. How was your day?"

"Busy. Strange."

"Strange?"

"Ever since I was promoted, everyone acts weird around me."

"What's strange about that? You're the boss now. No more fraternizing with the enlisted men."

I laughed, not expecting her to say something like that. "I'm the least bosslike person you'll ever meet."

"I bet you could get bossy."

"I don't know," I said. "It's not in me. So where are we eating?"

"I don't know," she said. "You're the boss."

I shook my head. "Tonight, you're the boss. It's your call."

"Okay," she said. "I'm taking you for pierogies. And I have the perfect place. I hope you're hungry."

"Famished," I said.

"Famished is perfect. You won't be when we're done."

We took the Blue Line to Belmont. As we got off the train, April took my hand and led me to a two-story brick building with a brass sign that read:

## Staropolska
### Polish American Cuisine

I opened the door and we stepped inside. The room was dark, woody and pungent. A small dark-haired woman in a floor-length skirt and apron greeted us with a heavy accent. "You are two?"

"Yes."

"This way, please."

"*Dziekuje*," April said.

I turned to April. "You speak Polish?"

"Just a few phrases. *Dziekuje* means 'thank you.' "

The restaurant had an old-world feel, with iron chandeliers, and bearskins on the wood-paneled walls.

Our hostess led us to a small table near the fireplace. A moment later our waitress came to the table. She put a basket of bread and a dish of some pale brown substance on the table. Then she handed us two menus. "What would you like to drink?" she asked.

"Do you like wine?" April asked me.

I nodded. "Yes, please."

"We would like some red wine. And water."

"With gas or still."

April looked at me.

"Remember, you're the boss," I said.

"Oh, yes," she said. "Sparkling."

The woman nodded. "I will come back in a moment," she said. She walked back to the kitchen.

"I think we're the only non-Poles in here," I said, looking around at the rest of the clientele.

"That's a good sign," she said. "If you want good Mexican food, you go where the Mexicans eat. You want good pierogies, find the Poles."

"So they're really that good?" I asked.

"Aside from Madame Curie, pierogies are the Poles' greatest contribution to humanity."

I looked at the menu. "They also have salmon."

"No salmon," she said. "I'll do the ordering tonight. I'm the boss. You said so yourself."

"You're right. But nothing too . . . different."

She gave me a smile that I knew meant she was about to ignore my request. "Trust me."

When our server came back, April was ready. "We'd like to start with zurek."

"That sounds like something on *Star Trek*," I said.

She shushed me.

Our server wrote on her pad of paper.

"And then?"

"The pierogi assortment with sausage, potato and sauerkraut. And then the Old Country Plate."

"You are hungry tonight," our waitress said.

"We are," April said, looking at me.

After our server left, April's eyes twinkled. "Are you excited?"

I'd never seen a woman get so excited about food. *Certainly not Ashley.* "Yes. Very."

"You should be." She scooped her knife into the pale brown substance and spread the mixture over a slice of bread, then took a bite. "Try some."

"Okay." I started spreading some over my bread. "What is it?"

"Smalec."

"That was helpful. Thank you."

She laughed. "It's lard."
I stopped spreading.
"Don't be a baby," she said, taking a bite. "It's good."
*Definitely not Ashley.*

Our server brought out the wine, left, then returned with our soup. The thick broth was grainy-looking, brownish gray and filled with sliced sausages and halved boiled eggs. I lifted a spoon and tasted it. It was flavorful but difficult to describe.

"What's this called?"

"Zurek. It's a sour rye soup."

"Sour rye?"

"Like sourdough. It also has boiled pork sausage. The Polish serve it on Easter. But it's good anytime. Especially when it's cold. Do you like it?"

"I do."

After we finished our soup, our server brought out two plates each with three dumplings. They were lightly browned and sprinkled with bacon. I poked one with my fork. "This does look like a gyoza."

There were three flavors of pierogies—potato and cheese, cabbage and barley, and spicy meat, covered in butter and bacon. All three were delicious.

The pierogies were as good as April had promised, and I was already full when our server brought out our main course, the Old Country Plate—a large platter with a charred link of kielbasa and a cabbage roll atop a bed of sauerkraut and a potato pancake.

"This is interesting," I said, prodding the cabbage with my fork.

"It's kind of like a stuffed pepper," she said.

The roll was savory, filled with spicy pork and rice.

"What do you think?" April asked.

"It's delicious. I should never have doubted you."

"No. You should never doubt your boss," she said. For the next several minutes we ate quietly. About halfway through the plate I had to stop. "This is too much food."

"The Polish like to eat hearty."

After we'd eaten as much as we could, our server returned to ask if we wanted dessert.

"I couldn't eat another bite," I said.

"No thank you," April said to the waitress. She turned to me. "But next time we'll try the blintzes."

"On our next tour?" I asked.

She nodded. "There's still so much of the city I need to show you."

"It's a big city. It could take months."

"Years," she said.

"Would you like coffee?" the waitress asked.

"Please," I said. "Decaf with milk."

"I'll have the same," April said.

While I drank my coffee April looked at me pensively—like she wanted to ask me something but was afraid to. Finally she said, "I like being with you."

I smiled. "I like being with you too."

She looked down for a moment. "May I ask you something personal?"

"Sure."

"I've thought a lot about what you told me last Saturday, about why you moved here. When you left your family behind, did you leave anyone else?"

"You mean, a girl?"

April frowned. "I'm sorry, that was forward of me." She must have noticed the pain on my face because she quickly added, "It's okay if you don't want to talk about it."

"Her name is Ashley."

"That's a pretty name," she said.

"Pretty girl," I said. "I thought we were going to get married. I had started looking for rings."

"What happened?"

"I moved to Chicago."

April looked puzzled. ". . . And?"

"And she stayed in Colorado."

She still looked perplexed. "She wouldn't follow you?"

"No," I said. "She wasn't happy that I was leaving Colorado."

"But she understood why you had to leave, right? For your brother."

"I never told her about my brother."

"Why not?"

"She didn't like my brother. If I had told her the truth, she would have exposed him, and he probably would have ended up in prison. Instead, I told her that I wanted something bigger than Denver. I know it's not honest, but I couldn't take a chance with my brother's life. Not that it mattered. She really didn't want to get married anyway."

April was quiet a moment then said, "Ashley's a fool."

Heading back on the train, we were both quiet. My thoughts were completely magnetized to what she'd said about Ashley. Or what she'd meant by it.

We arrived at the Irving Park station a little after eleven.

"May I walk you to your apartment?" I asked.

She nodded. "I'd like that."

I got off the train with her and we walked down the stairway.

"I wonder how many Poles there are in Chicago?" I said.

"Someone told me that Chicago is the second-largest Polish city in the world—second only to Warsaw. I don't know if that's true, but I wouldn't doubt it." She looked at me. "So, do you feel more Polish?"

"I definitely feel more Polish than I did this morning."

"You look more Polish," she said.

I grinned. "How do I look more Polish?"

"You look happier."

"Do I?"

"Much happier than when I first met you."

"I'm sure that's true. Are Poles happy?"

"They invented the polka didn't they?"

"You've got a point."

Walking beneath the elevated track, the train makes a

horrible, frightening sound, like a dragon's screech. I wondered if Chicagoans even noticed it. I wondered how long it would be before I didn't notice it anymore.

Holding hands, we walked west on Irving Park Road to Keeler, against traffic on the one-way street that led to April's apartment. The closer we got to her apartment, the quieter she became. At her doorstep she was suddenly acting shy, more like a teenage girl on a first date than a woman. She looked into my eyes. "That was really fun."

"You give really good tours," I said.

"Thank you. I like giving you tours."

"What are you doing this Saturday?"

"I don't know," she said, looking down. A few seconds later she said, "Hopefully, spending it with you."

"I would like that," I said. "Saturday morning?"

She nodded. As we looked into each other's eyes, I couldn't believe how impossibly beautiful she was. But what I was seeing seemed to be more than just physical beauty. It was the unique space she held in the universe. She had an indefinable sweetness and femininity and maternal nature that made me want to cling to her and never let go.

From the look in her eyes, I knew she too was feeling something powerful—the two of us drawn together by feelings stronger than either of us. I leaned forward and gently pressed my lips against hers. At first she just stood there, awkwardly, unsure, then she surrendered, returning my kisses. I put my arms around her and pulled her tightly into me, our kisses growing still deeper.

We kissed for several minutes, then suddenly she pushed me away. "Stop."

"What?" I said.

"I'm sorry," she said, looking down. "I'm so sorry." She didn't sound angry. She sounded frustrated. Like me. She looked back up at me as her eyes welled up with tears. "I'm really sorry."

She leaned forward and kissed me on the cheek. Then she opened her door and went inside, leaving me standing in the hallway, wondering what had just happened.

# CHAPTER

## *Sixteen*

*I dreamed that I was at a ritzy party held in a swanky mansion. I had just taken an hors d'oeuvre from a server when I noticed a beautiful woman standing alone across the room staring at me. With one finger she gestured for me to come to her. Something about her eyes frightened me, but still I obeyed. As I stepped forward I saw she was standing in the middle of a giant spider web. The web behind her was lined with silk cocoons, most of which were still, though some of them were moving as the occupant struggled hopelessly to escape. I turned to run from her when I too found myself ensnared in her web. I looked back to see her coming toward me. I woke screaming, tangled in my sheets.*

✦ Joseph Jacobson's Diary ✦

I called April three times the next day, Thursday, but she didn't answer. With each unanswered call I grew more frustrated. *What was going on? What had I done wrong? Was she ever going to talk to me again?* The idea of another rejection was too much to consider. I needed to know what had gone wrong. I needed to see her again. Friday morning I decided I would leave work early and catch her at the diner.

A half-hour before noon there was a knock on my door. Before I could get up, the door opened and Potts's fiancée, Brandi, stuck her head in. "Anyone home?"

I hadn't seen her since my first day at the agency. I was surprised to see her. "Hi," I said.

"May I come in?"

"Things are a mess. We've been so busy . . ."

"I know," she said, shutting the door behind her. "Peter told me that he had promoted you." She walked up to my desk and reached out her perfectly manicured hand. "We were never properly introduced. My name is Brandi."

"I'm Joseph. Or J.J."

"J.J.," she said, smiling. She was still holding my hand. "Sounds like a rapper."

I casually withdrew my hand. "I've heard that."

"What does your mother call you?"

"Joseph."

"I'll call you that," she said. "So, Joseph, Peter said you saved an account your first day at work."

"I got lucky."

"It's good to get lucky," she said, looking me in the eyes. She sat on my desk. "Then again, maybe it's not so lucky."

"What do you mean?"

"You're setting the expectations too high. What do you do for an encore, save the world?"

I grinned. "You might be right."

"I usually am," she said wryly. "So where in the world are you from?"

"Denver."

"Mile-High City," she said. "So, what do you think of the Windy City?"

"It's big," I said. "I'm still learning my way around."

"I can point you to all the hot spots," she said. "What do you do for fun?"

"Not much, lately," I said.

"I can help with that. We should get together for a drink sometime." She hesitated just a moment before adding, ". . . Or something."

I pretended not to hear her addendum. She just gazed

at me like she was reading a magazine. When the silence started to get uncomfortable, she said, "So what do you think of the big agency life?"

"It's exciting," I said.

"You'll get over it," she said. "You know, you still have that deer-in-the-headlamps look about you. But it's kind of cute. I like that in a man. It's very sexy."

"You like what in a man?" I asked.

"Vulnerability."

"Peter doesn't strike me as the vulnerable type."

She bit her lower lip, then leaned forward toward me, looking me in the eyes. "All men are vulnerable. You've just got to find the right kryptonite."

I just stared at her, tongue-tied.

Suddenly, she leaned back and laughed. "Don't be so serious." She stood back up. "I better go." She walked to my office door, then stopped and looked me up and down. "See you around, Joseph."

"Bye," I said.

She shut the door behind her.

*No, no, no,* I thought.

Minutes after she left I gathered my things in my backpack and went to find Timothy. He was sitting at his cubicle sketching with one of the Leo Burnett big black pencils.

"Hey, Timothy."

He looked up. "Yeah, what's up?"

"I've got to take an extra long lunch today. Can you, like, take care of things?"

He just looked at me.

"I know, stupid question. Will you cover for me?"

"Sure. When will you be back?"

"Two hours. I need to run home. I'll stay late to make it up."

"You've stayed late every night this week," Timothy said. "Just work through lunch, then leave early."

"Are you okay with that?"

"You're the boss," Timothy said.

"In name only."

He grinned. "Don't worry. Potts is leaving early. His squeeze came by."

"Yeah, I know," I said, sighing.

"What does that mean?"

"She paid me a visit. Invited me out for a drink . . . or whatever."

He grimaced. "I would steer clear of that reef, my friend. Head for deep waters."

"Thanks for the advice."

"Anytime. Have a good weekend."

"I hope so."

I worked another hour, then left, reaching the Jefferson Park station by one. My heart was filled with apprehension. April worked at the diner until two on Fridays. I would reach her just about the time she got off. I could wait outside if I had to. I hoped there wouldn't be a scene.

It was ten to two when I entered the diner's front door. There were only a half-dozen people inside and the only waitress in the front was Ewa, a tall blond Polish woman at least ten years older than me. April had told me that they were friends, but we'd never been introduced. Ewa said with a Polish accent, "Just sit anywhere you . . ." She paused. "No, you are here for April."

"Yes. Is she here?"

She nodded hesitantly. "She's in back."

"Could you tell her I'm here, please."

She just looked at me, her eyes narrowing threateningly. "You be careful. I will get her, but you be careful with her. She is a good girl."

"I wouldn't hurt her."

"Maybe you hurt her without trying," she said. "You be careful." She walked back into the kitchen. It was a couple minutes before April walked out. She looked embarrassed and vulnerable.

"Hi," she said softly.

"Hi."

She didn't say anything.

"Why haven't you been taking my calls?"

"I'm sorry."

I waited for some kind of explanation, but she didn't offer one.

"I came by to see if we were still on for tomorrow. For our tour."

"They're not tours, they're dates."

"So, they're dates. Is there something wrong with that?"
She didn't answer.

After a minute I exhaled heavily. "Look, I have no idea what happened. I thought there was something between us. If I did or said something to hurt you, I'm really sorry. I know we've just met, but I really care about you. I would never hurt you intentionally." I waited for her to say something, but she didn't. I exhaled in frustration. "Look, if you don't want to see me, just tell me. I won't bother you again." She still just looked at me, tears welling up in her eyes. Finally, I said, "All right. I won't make you say it." I turned to go.

"Wait," she said, her voice cracking.

I looked back at her. She was crying.

"Please don't go. I want to see you."

I took a step closer to her. "April, what's going on?"

"I can't tell you." She wiped her eyes. "I wish I could, but I can't. But we'll date, okay? We'll get to know each other."

"I don't understand."

"I know. But I just need time. We'll have fun. I promise. I'll be good to you." She reached out and took my hand. "I really want to be with you. I'm sorry I'm so hard. Please don't give up on me."

I looked into her pleading eyes, feeling the warmth of her hand in mine. I took a deep breath. "I won't give up on you. And I won't ask what's going on." I tilted my head. "But there's one thing I need to know."

She looked at me anxiously. "What?"

"You're not an outlaw, are you?"

A broad smile crossed her face. "No."

"Good. Because I don't want to end up in court someday testifying against you."

She laughed, then she hugged me. "I'm going to make you so happy you came to Chicago."

# C H A P T E R

## *Seventeen*

*It is impossible to build a solid foundation on the sand of the unkown.*

✦ Joseph Jacobson's Diary ✦

My high school football coach used to say, "Men, sometimes you gotta walk through Hell to get to Heaven." I was beginning to believe him. As difficult as being thrown out of Colorado had been, I was actually starting to feel grateful that it had happened. I never would have met April if I hadn't left home. My job at Leo Burnett was fulfilling. My Bank On It campaign was a big success, and April never failed to point out the BankOne billboards we passed. She even cut out BankOne ads she saw in newspapers or magazines.

The next eight months were not what I expected when I first arrived in Chicago. They were good. A better word would be "idyllic." April and I grew closer, to the point I couldn't imagine being without her.

I finally met April's roommate, Ruth. She was not what I expected—practically a photographic negative of April. The evening I met her she was wearing a torn Nirvana T-shirt revealing the tattoos on her arms and neck. She had tattoos on her face and at least a dozen piercings. She wore small safety pins in her ears.

She was friendly and soft-spoken, like April, but otherwise the two couldn't have been a more incongruous pair.

After we left the apartment, I asked April, "How did you two meet?"

"She's an old friend," she said. "From Utah."

The route April took from Mr. G's to the Jefferson Park station led past my apartment, so I gave her a key to my place so she could save the trip home and wait at my place after her shift on the evenings we planned to go out. She began stopping by and cleaning my place or bringing me food from the diner and leaving it in my refrigerator, usually with a love note.

I remembered what my father had said about love—"You'll know it's love when you don't have to ask." I now understood what he meant. With Ashley, my heart was always asking. It seemed to me that with her, love was an emotional shell game. With April there was no such doubt. I wasn't so much *in love* as love was *in me.* I felt it all the time with her; in every phone call, every smile, every frown of concern.

In July, I came down with the flu for a week and she barely left my side, bringing me soup from the diner, doing my laundry and picking up my medications. She seemed grateful for the chance to take care of me. The inverse was true too. I wanted to make her happy. Ashley was right. For better or worse, I was a pleaser. And pleasers tend to become doormats for those with different sensibilities. April was also a pleaser. We were perfect together. I'd never been closer to anyone in my life.

Nor had I ever known anyone who was more honest, which was the greatest irony of our relationship. She simultaneously hid nothing present and everything past. It was as if a big curtain had been drawn over the largest part of her life.

Most of the time it was possible to ignore the curtain. But every now and then something would slip out, and I would be reminded that there was something about her I didn't know—something, perhaps, that could take her away from me.

I learned one more thing. April was highly susceptible to guilt, and whatever it was she was hiding was definitely eating at her. At those times she would pray more and read her Bible and sometimes fast. She would put boundaries between us physically. These times would remind me that even in Eden there were snakes.

April's birthday came in August. On Timothy's recommendation, I took her to the Berghoff, one of Chicago's oldest and most famous restaurants. At dinner I gave her my gift, a silver chain with a Tiffany heart lock pendant in sterling silver with Tiffany Blue enamel finish. She squealed when she saw it. She asked me to put it on her. After that I never saw her without it.

Summer slipped into fall, and fall into winter. As the weather cooled and the holidays approached, I could feel something happening between April and me as well. Relationships either grow or die, but they never stay the same. We'd come to a place of decision. I had already made mine. I wanted to take this to the next step. I didn't care about what I didn't know, or at least I didn't think I did. I couldn't imagine anything that would change the way I felt about her. What I knew for certain is that I couldn't imagine a world without her. Whatever she was hiding, we were going to make this work.

The day before Thanksgiving, Timothy reminded everyone about the upcoming Leo Burnett Holiday Formal in mid-December—one of the highlights of the company's year. Timothy summed up the event with two words. "Legendary. Epic."

Thanksgiving came and though I was homesick, I was not without company. I helped April cook Thanksgiving dinner, which we shared with Ruth and her boyfriend, Bob, who, compared to Ruth, looked surprisingly normal.

The dinner was good, but April was acting quiet again and there was sadness in her eyes. Her sadness made me afraid. It hadn't really been that long since Ashley had thrown me aside. I had been wrong before. Who was to say I wasn't wrong now? Had April stopped loving me? Or had the specter of her past returned to claim her?

After dinner I told April about the Leo Burnett Christmas party. She was even more excited than I thought she'd be. "I've never been to anything like that before," she said. "Ruth has some beautiful dresses I could borrow." She kissed me. "They're a little, uh, showy, at least for me, but I don't think you'll mind."

I smiled. "I doubt it."

Weeks passed and December brought an earnest chill. The cold even seemed to creep into our relationship. Relationships, by nature, require trust, and trust cannot grow in the fog of secrecy. Whether it was paranoia or the nature of our circumstance, April seemed different to me. I was afraid I was losing her. And fear is the most untrustworthy of counselors.

Fear demanded that I know where we were going, and I couldn't know that, I couldn't trust that, without knowing where she'd been. She needed to come clean about her past. No more secrets. She needed to tell me everything.

On December 7, a week before the Leo Burnett party, I decided to make her tell me.

# CHAPTER

## Eighteen

*Is it wisdom to search out what will hurt us most?*
*Is painful truth better than ignorant bliss?*

✦ Joseph Jacobson's Diary ✦

It was a Friday night when I decided to force April's hand. Even though we were at our favorite sushi restaurant, I had hardly eaten. Neither of us had. It was my fault. I was quiet and upset, and April was reflecting my emotions.

Finally she asked, "Are you okay?"

"No."

She gazed at me expectantly. "Did I do something wrong?"

I took my napkin off my lap and set it on the table. "We need to talk."

Her eyes began to well up with tears. "Are you breaking up with me?"

"No," I said. I looked down for a moment, then said, "I can't do this anymore, April. I need to know who I'm in love with."

She looked at me fearfully. "I'm not sure how to tell you."

"Just tell me the truth, and we'll deal with it."

She sat there quietly for a moment. Then she said, "You know I love you, right?"

I exhaled slowly. "That's what they always say before they leave you."

She reached over for my hand. "I'm not leaving you. But you might leave me."

"I would never leave you."

"You don't know that."

She looked fearfully in my eyes, then said, "Okay." She took a deep breath. "I'm married."

"What?"

"I'm not with him anymore, but I'm still married."

"You're separated?"

"Yes . . ."

"But you're getting divorced?"

Her brow fell. "It's not that simple." She looked up at me. "I'm not saying divorce is simple. But . . ." She sighed. "I'm afraid to tell you."

"Why?"

"Because I'm afraid I'll freak you out."

"What could *you* possibly have done that would freak me out?"

She was quiet for nearly a minute, then she said, "Remember, you made me do this."

The way she said that frightened me. "I know."

She swallowed. "Remember when you told me you come from a large family?"

"Yes."

"So do I. There are thirty-six of us."

"Thirty-six?"

"My father was married five times."

I wasn't sure where she was going with this. "Well, he's only got one marriage on my father."

". . . At the same time."

It took me a moment for comprehension to set in. "He's polygamous?"

"That little town I'm from in southern Utah is called Hill-dale. It's a polygamist colony."

She looked into my eyes nervously. "I followed in my parents' footsteps. I got married when I was eighteen. I'm the fourth wife of five."

I had no idea what to say.

April looked frightened. After a couple minutes she said, "Please say something."

"I don't know how to respond to that."

She reached across the table and took my hand. "Please don't leave me."

"I'm not . . . I just . . ." I exhaled. "Wow. That's nothing I've ever encountered." I looked at her. "Or imagined I'd encounter." I sat there quietly processing. "You left him?"

She nodded. "We all did. At least four of us did."

"What happened?"

"This will sound a little strange to you." She hesitated. "Actually, probably a *lot* strange. John, my husband, is fifty-three. Two years ago the Elders of our church gave him another wife, Elizabeth. She was only seventeen. Elizabeth didn't want to marry a fifty-three-year-old man. Especially since she had a boyfriend her same age. So, a couple days before John was to marry her, Elizabeth and her boyfriend ran away together. John was crushed. He felt so bad that after a few weeks the wives got together and told him he should go to Salt Lake and visit a polygamous family we knew with five daughters.

"He came back from Salt Lake with Lindsay, a beautiful little nineteen-year-old blonde. John was as giddy as a honeymooner. The next few weeks we barely saw him. He was always with her. She had him wrapped around her finger.

"When she realized how much control she had over him, she began to manipulate him. She became a little tyrant. She would scream at us and give us orders. Once, she got mad at me and pulled my hair. I went to John, but he wouldn't even listen to me.

"The turning point came when John whited out his first wife's name from their marriage certificate."

"Whited out?"

"Because polygamous marriages aren't recognized by the state, we only have one marriage certificate—the first wife. John's first wife is named Andrea. She's the same age he is. They kept that marriage certificate framed on the wall of their bedroom. John took some Wite-Out and painted over Andrea's name, then wrote in Lindsay's. That's when Andrea threw them both out. So, for the next year, it was the four of us. We took care of each other.

"But a year ago John said he was taking the house back, so we all left. I came to Chicago because Ruth invited me to be her roommate. She left the colony a couple years earlier."

"Ruth was a polygamist's wife?"

April nodded.

"I never would have guessed that."

"Sometimes when people leave a belief system, they go to the opposite extreme. It happens a lot."

I put my head in my hands.

"What are you thinking?" she asked.

"I'm just mentally treading water," I said. "I don't know what to think about this." After a minute I looked up at her. "How do you get a divorce when you were never legally married?"

"It has to be done with the church. But I left the church, so there's no finality."

"The Mormon church?"

She shook her head. "No. Mormons haven't practiced polygamy for more than a century. I belong to a fundamentalist group."

We both sat there, not knowing what to say. As the silence grew uncomfortable, tears began to fall down her cheeks again.

"I don't blame you if you leave me. But please don't. I love you."

"I just need time to sort things out."

She wiped her eyes with her napkin. "I understand."

I stood. "Come on. Let's go."

"No," she said. "You go. You need to think."

"I'll call you," I said. "Tomorrow."

She looked at me doubtfully. "Okay."

I stopped at the front counter and paid the bill, then walked out the door alone. My mind was reeling. Finally, everything made sense. And nothing did.

# CHAPTER

## Nineteen

*Sometimes our cruelest acts come not from meaning to do wrong but from not trying hard enough not to.*

✦ Joseph Jacobson's Diary ✦

I didn't call April the next day. Or the next. I didn't call her that whole week. It's not that I wasn't thinking about her—I couldn't stop thinking about her—it's just that I wasn't sure what to say if I did. I didn't even send the text messages I had written. It may sound strange coming from a professional copywriter, but I just couldn't find the right words.

At first I told myself that I didn't know who she really was. But the truth was, I knew exactly who she was. She was the woman I loved. As incomprehensible as her past was to me, it had also made her one of the kindest, sweetest women I had ever met. I suppose it was hypocritical of me to love the fruit but hate the tree.

It took me a full week to sort things out, to realize the truth that whatever she was born into didn't matter. I wasn't interested in her past. I didn't even have a past anymore. I was living for the future and I wanted her in it.

I thought it best to tell her what I'd discovered in person, so I decided to tell her on Friday—the night of the Christmas party.

If you're a woman reading this, you won't understand my thinking. I've been told it's a guy thing. Or maybe it was just the way I was raised by my father—*stick to the plan until you hear differently*—but it never occurred to me that April might not be expecting me the night of our company Christmas party. After all, I had never told her we wouldn't be going.

I called the morning of the party to let her know what time I'd pick her up. But she didn't answer. I assumed she was busy and left a message.

Around six o'clock I took a cab to April's apartment. I knocked on her door, but she didn't answer. I knocked again. Then I called her cell phone, but it went right to messages. I walked back out to the cab and climbed in.

"Take me to Lawrence and Austin," I said. "Mr. G's Diner."

Ten minutes later the driver pulled up to the diner's curb. "Shall I wait?"

"Yes. I'll only be a minute."

The diner was crowded as it usually was on the weekend. Ewa was standing behind the counter. She watched me enter.

"Hello, Joseph," she said. Her tone was angry.

"Have you seen April?"

"She's gone."

"Gone where?"

"She went back to Utah."

My chest constricted with panic. "When did she leave?"

"Yesterday."

"Yesterday?"

"I told you to be careful. She was very, very sad that you did not call her. She cried for many days. You broke her heart."

"I didn't mean . . ." I exhaled. "I just tried to call her, but she wouldn't answer. Would you please call her for me?"

Ewa shook her head. "She did not take her phone. She said she would not need it there. Just a minute." She walked out of the kitchen door, then returned. "She left this for you." She lay something on the counter. It was the Tiffany necklace I'd given April for her birthday. My heart felt like it would break.

"How do I find her?" I asked.

Ewa looked at me as if she was amazed by my stupidity. "You cannot find her. She went back to her husband."

My head spun. I could hardly breathe I was so sick with grief—much worse than when Ashley had told me she wasn't going to follow me. This time I was to blame. *Why hadn't I just called? How could I have been so stupid?*

I just stood there, my world caving in around me. After a minute Ewa said, "We are busy, I must go. I am sorry for you." She disappeared into the kitchen.

I stood there for a moment, stunned, until I noticed several diners in the restaurant looking at me. I picked up the necklace and put it in my pocket. Then, on weak legs, I walked back out to the taxi.

"Not there?" the driver asked as I shut the door.

"No," I said. Even though I was just a few blocks from my apartment, I didn't want to go back. The idea of being alone terrified me. I handed him the invitation to the party. "Just take me to this address."

# CHAPTER

## Twenty

*The spider has spun her web.*

✦ Joseph Jacobson's Diary ✦

The company Christmas party was held at a 10,000-square-foot mansion in the Kenilworth suburb of Chicago—the home of Leo Burnett Chicago's CEO, Mr. Grant. As we drove through the massive iron gates and up the cobblestone driveway, the lane looked like the sales lot of a luxury car dealership. It was filled with shiny Lamborghinis, Bentleys, Aston-Martins, Porsches, BMWs, Mercedeses, and Cadillacs. Parked near the front door was Mr. Grant's bright orange Maserati.

"Nice place," the driver said.

"Yeah." I handed him two twenties.

"Call me if you need a ride back," he said, handing me his card.

I walked up to the giant carved-oak doors, which were decorated with oversized Christmas wreaths adorned with gold and ivory ribbons and baubles.

One of the knickered valets opened the door for me as I approached. "Welcome," he said. "Have a good evening."

I mumbled, "Thank you."

My senses were flooded by the home's ambience. The home was gaily lit, and the powerful fragrance of cinnamon, peppermint and clove filled the foyer. Christmas trees lined the entryway walls like a forest, and the stair railing was wrapped in fresh garland twinkling with gold Christmas lights. In a small, open room off the foyer, a string quartet accompanied by a pianist on an electric piano played Pachelbel's Canon in D. I listened to them for a moment, then panned the rest of the room for the bar. I desperately needed a drink.

I spotted Timothy standing near a buffet table. I started to make my way to him but was stopped by Peter, who was wearing his signature black silk tee beneath an all-silver suit, iridescent as fish scales. Brandi was holding on to his arm. She was even more stunning than usual, wearing a sheer, low-cut gown, tight at the waist with a slit in front exposing her long, slender legs. Both of them were carrying stemmed glasses half-full of white wine. From Peter's inebriated glow I could tell he'd started drinking long before my arrival.

"Hey, J.J.J.," Peter said. "Where's your date?"

"She's not here," I said.

"We can see that," Peter said.

"She couldn't make it."

Brandi cocked her head. "Aww, that's sad."

I ignored her molesting eyes. "How's the party?"

"Good booze," Peter said, eyeing two women as they walked past us. "See you."

Brandi smiled at me as he pulled her away. "Ciao."

A butler walked up to me. "May I take your coat, sir?"

"Sure." I took it off and handed it to him. He ascended the

circular staircase with my coat draped over his arm. Timothy had disappeared, but I saw Kim standing next to the buffet table in the dining room.

The long, rectangular table was crowded with the most decadent spread I had ever seen: shrimp and crab bowls, sushi, pâté de foie gras, little cream pastries, hand-dipped chocolates, meringues, cherry-topped macaroons and at least six different tarts. In the center of the table was an ice sculpture of our agency's initials, set between two thick red candles.

"Hi, Kim," I said.

She looked relieved to see me. "Joseph. When did you get here?"

"Just now."

"Where's April?"

"She couldn't make it," I said, trying to hide the emotion in my voice. "Something came up."

"She's missing out," Kim said. "Grab a plate. The food's fantastic."

Even though I wasn't hungry, I took a plate and began filling it with food.

"Are you okay?" Kim asked.

"My father holds a Christmas party this same night," I said. "This is the first time in sixteen years I won't be attending."

"I'm sorry to hear that," she said.

Just then a man I didn't know walked up to her and she turned to talk to him. I drifted to another room with a Strass crystal chandelier and ivory carpets and a grand piano. Sade and Chloe were seated near the doorway, drinking and laughing. Kate was standing next to her boyfriend, who was playing a Billy Joel song on the piano.

"J.J.!" Chloe said. "Come visit us." She sounded a little tipsy.

"Hey, J.J.," Kate said.

"Hi, Kate."

"This is my boyfriend, Clark." He nodded a little, in time with the music.

"Look," Sade said, holding a sprig of parsley from the buffet table. "Mistletoe."

"What are you drinking?" I asked.

"Eggnog."

"Very strong eggnog," Chloe said.

"Aren't you going to kiss me?" Sade said.

"Sure." I gave her a quick peck.

"Where's your girlfriend?" Kate asked.

"She bailed on me," I said.

She looked at me sympathetically. "I'm sorry."

"Me too."

"I'll be your girlfriend tonight," Chloe said.

"Chloe," Sade said sharply. "Stop it. You're drunk."

"I'm not drunk," she said. "And you're the one who got a kiss."

"I think it's time for me to go," I said.

Kate nodded in agreement, shaking her head at Chloe.

"Oh, don't go," Chloe said.

I kissed her on the cheek. "Sorry." I said to Clark, "Nice to meet you."

"Likewise."

"Merry Christmas," I said to everyone, then walked out of the room. I left my plate of untouched food on a small end table. I found the taxi driver's card in my pocket and called. The taxi was only ten minutes out, so I started looking around for the coat man. When I couldn't find him, I walked upstairs to retrieve my coat myself.

The coats were laid out on the carpeted floor of a massive bedroom at the top of the stairway, with a dozen or so furs layered on top of each other across the bed. There were at least a hundred coats and finding mine wasn't as simple as I thought it would be.

As I foraged through a pile of coats, Brandi walked into the room.

"Hi, J.J.," she said. She carried two glasses of wine. "Would you like a drink?" She sounded a little drunk, which didn't surprise me.

"No thank you."

"Oh, come on. I brought it for you."

I looked past her to the door. "Where's Peter?"

"Who cares?" she said. She shut the door with her hip. "Have your drink."

I looked at her warily. "I was just looking for my coat. I've got to go. My cab's on its way."

"And leave me here all by my lonesome?" She took a few more steps toward me. "I don't want to be alone. C'mon, Joseph. Just drink with me. It's Christmas."

"I can't," I said.

"Can't or won't."

"Both," I said. "You're engaged to Peter."

"We're not doing anything wrong." She took a sip of her wine and smiled. "At least not yet. You can feel guilty later."

"Peter's my friend. He trusts me."

"Peter's not your friend. And why do you keep bringing him up? I don't see him in here." She took another step closer and set her glass on the nightstand. She dipped her finger in the other wineglass and held it up to my lips. "Try it. It's delicious."

"Brandi, don't."

She sucked the wine off her own finger. "Do you know how many men want me?"

"Millions."

"But not you? Are you one in a million, Mr. Joseph Jacobson? You don't want me?"

"I want Mr. Grant's Maserati, but I'm not going to steal it."

"You don't have to steal it," she said. "You can just take it for a ride." She put her hand on my shoulder. "And you just compared me to a car." She smiled seductively. "Are you objectifying me, Mr. J.J.?"

"I'm just saying that I don't take what's not mine."

"You are objectifying me. You see me as someone's possession." A broad smile crossed her face. "Don't worry, I like being objectified." She set the second glass down on the nightstand. "I may be an object, but I'm not anyone's possession. I am free to give myself to whomever I choose." She pointed at me. "And, right now, I choose you."

"Brandi, you're drunk."

"I'm not drunk. If I were drunk, I would have done something really crazy, like ripped open my dress. Like this." She grabbed the top of her dress and pulled it open, exposing her brassiere. "Then I would have just thrown myself at you. Like this." She pulled me on top of her over a padding of fur coats. "We should do it on mink."

"We're not doing anything," I said, pushing away from her.

"Yes we are."

At that moment the door opened. "Brandi?" Peter stood in the doorway staring at us, trying to figure out what he was seeing. "What are you doing?" His words were slurred.

Brandi immediately started pushing me away. "Stop it! Get off of me!" As I stood, she looked over at Peter. "Your employee attacked me." She pointed to her breast. "Look, he ripped my dress."

"That's not what happened," I said.

Peter charged up to me, his face red with fury. "You son of a—" His fist crashed against my jaw, knocking me back.

"Peter, stop it," I said. "She came after me."

"Liar!" Brandi shouted. "He tried to rape me."

"That's a lie."

"Don't talk to my woman like that," Peter shouted, swinging wildly. I didn't fight back. Instead, I just put my arms up to protect myself. Still, he knocked me to the ground.

"Peter. I didn't do anything."

"You stay there," he shouted, pointing at me with a trembling finger. "You stay there, you lying . . ." He stopped as if unable to find a suitable word to describe me.

I just looked up at him from the floor.

Brandi stood behind him, grabbing his arms and staring hatefully at me. "Thank goodness you came when you did."

"Peter, it wasn't me," I said. "You know it."

"Shut up," Peter said. "Just shut up."

Then I saw him wipe his eyes. He knew I was telling the truth. He had to know I was telling the truth.

The two of them walked out. I still couldn't find my coat, so I left without it. I grabbed a handful of snow outside and held it to my jaw as I got into the cab.

"You okay?" the driver asked.

"Best night of my life," I said.

# CHAPTER

## Twenty-one

*Fate, like fire, is not selective about what it will consume.*

✦ Joseph Jacobson's Diary ✦

I passed the weekend in a coma of despair. I must have watched at least eighteen hours of television. I didn't eat anything except a bag of potato chips, which I downed with at least a dozen beers. *Why was this happening to me?*

Monday morning came too early. The sky was overcast as if mirroring the dread that filled my heart. I wasn't at my desk for more than five minutes when my phone buzzed. "I want to see you in my office," Peter said.

"All right," I said, even though he'd already hung up.

I walked to his office. Kim looked at me sympathetically, a very bad sign.

"Peter paged me," I said.

"Just go in," she said softly.

I stepped inside his office. He sat behind his desk, staring at me with disgust. I didn't know what Peter was going to do, but from his expression, I had a pretty good idea.

"I want your resignation."

I looked at him a moment, then shook my head. "No. I didn't do anything wrong."

"Are you calling my fiancée a cheater or a liar?"

*Pick one,* I thought. I said nothing.

"And don't tell me she came up to the room to seduce you."

"She just had too much to drink, she . . ." I looked in his face. He was shaking with anger and the veins in his forehead bulged. ". . . Actually, that's exactly what happened."

He stood up, pushing his chair back in the motion. He gestured wildly with his finger. "If we weren't in this office right now, I'd break you into a thousand pieces."

"Then it's a good thing we're in this office," I said coolly.

He glared at me for a moment, then said, "I can't fire you. But I can have you demoted and transferred."

"On what grounds," I said. "Your fiancée attempting to seduce me?"

Peter pounded his desk hard, so hard I thought its glass cover would break. "You say that again and this office won't protect you."

"I'm not your enemy, Peter."

His eyes narrowed. "And Brandi is?"

I didn't answer him. Her unfaithfulness was clearly too much for him to handle. I sat down in the chair in front of his desk. "You need to calm down."

"I didn't tell you to sit."

I just looked at him.

"I don't need H.R. approval to transfer you. I'm sending you to our New York office—unless you decide to resign. Either works for me. Make your choice."

I couldn't believe that I was being banished again. Still,

banishment or not, I couldn't stay in Chicago. Potts would make my life miserable. I should say *more* miserable. I had lost April. I was already suffering.

"I'll go to New York," I said.

"Good riddance," he said. He pulled his chair forward and sat.

"Whom do I report to?"

"Ask Kim. Now get out of my office."

I walked to the door. I hesitated just a moment, then turned back and walked toward Peter's desk.

"My father was big on self-defense," I said. "He insisted that all of his boys be able to take care of themselves. I have two black belts and I used to be ranked nationally. When I was nineteen, I competed in an open ultimate fighting competition on a dare and won.

"For the record, you swing like an eight-year-old boy. The only reason I didn't beat you to a pulp on Friday is because I know what it's like to have the woman you love hurt you."

Peter just stared at me.

"You're a bully, Potts. And there are few things in this world more satisfying than watching a bully get his comeuppance. So, if you still want to 'break me into a thousand pieces,' come and get me. And don't use the office excuse, I won't tell anyone. Except to get you some help."

He knew I was telling the truth. I could tell by the fear in his eyes.

After a moment I slowly shook my head. "I thought so.

Most bullies are cowards. You're a coward, Potts. And a fool. You'll eventually get yours. And you'll learn the truth about Brandi, no matter how many messengers you kill. Good luck with that."

He didn't say a word as I walked out of his office.

# CHAPTER

## *Twenty-two*

*I dreamt I woke in a train. Not only did not I know where it was going, I didn't even know where in the world I was. I got off at the first stop in what appeared to be a small, third world country. Asia? South America? I wasn't sure. I asked for a ticket to Colorado, but the person at the ticket counter couldn't understand me. I remember saying, "I think I'm lost."*

✦. Joseph Jacobson's Diary .✦

The H.R. people at Burnett were efficient at moving their people, and Wednesday morning, just a week before Christmas, I was on a flight to LaGuardia. Then again, maybe Peter had just expedited things because he was scared I might change my mind and come back for him.

I rented, sight unseen, a relatively inexpensive studio apartment in Sunnyside, in western Queens. I could be in downtown Manhattan in fifteen minutes if I took the No. 7 train.

Leo Burnett New York was located near Madison Square Park on Park Avenue South, a street that paralleled the famed advertising mecca of Madison Avenue.

I took a cab from the airport directly to the agency, carrying my bags into the building with me. I took the elevator to the seventh floor and sat in an austere waiting room for about an hour waiting to see the company H.R. director—a middle-aged woman with a broad, clamlike mouth bent in a scowl.

"Joseph Jacobson," she said, looking over my file. "Another transfer from our Chicago office. I don't know why they keep sending us their dross."

"I can hear you," I said.

She didn't respond. "You're in what department?"

"Copy."

"Just a minute." She flipped through a directory a moment, then, lifting the phone receiver, looked back up. "What's your name again?"

"It's Joseph Jacobson."

"Joseph," she said. She dialed a number. "Hi. I have a Joseph Jacobson in my office. He says he was just hired in Copy. Okay. Okay. Go ahead." Long pause. "All right, I'll give him the address." She set down the phone and looked up at me. "You're at the wrong location," she said. "You're supposed to be at the Seventh Avenue office."

"You have more than one office?"

"We have a satellite office." She wrote down the address on the back of a business card and handed it to me. "That's where you need to go."

I walked back out to the street, dragging my luggage behind me. My destination was about twelve blocks from the main office, and I dragged my luggage through the crowds of tourists that flooded the city at Christmastime.

The satellite office was located in a tired, dingy building, and the only indication of its connection with the Park Avenue office was a diminutive brass sign on the wall inside the lobby. A tall, middle-aged woman was sitting at the reception desk. "You must be Joseph," she said.

"Yes I am."

"I'm Charlene. Welcome to the think tank."

"Is that what they call it?" I asked.

"Yes. But we call it the sink tank. Sometimes the stink tank."

I looked around the office. It was small, maybe a thousand square feet. The eggshell white walls were simply decorated with framed pictures of advertisements in black steel frames. There was a small Christmas tree decorated with baubles, lights and tiny plastic Menorahs.

"Why aren't we near the rest of the agency?" I asked.

"This is corporate Siberia. This is where they send you while they're deciding your fate. If you're here, someone doesn't like you."

"Then I'm in the right place. What is it that we do here?"

"We do what no one else wants to do. Write copy for the back of cereal boxes, direct mail pieces, the mundane stuff."

"Where is everyone else?"

"There's only four of us right now. You, me, Bryce and Leonard."

"Leonard," I said. "Is he blond, thin and wears wire-rimmed glasses? Calls himself Len?"

"You got three out of four," she said. "Not so thin."

"Did he come here from the Chicago office?"

"About a year ago. Come to think of it, he was thin back then."

"I wondered where they had sent him," I said.

"So you're from Chicago too."

"Most recently. Actually, I'm from Colorado. Chicago was just a stop on my way up the ladder," I said facetiously.

Just then the door opened and two men walked in. One

was a short, smartly dressed African-American man. The other was Leonard—though it took me a moment to recognize him as he had probably put on thirty pounds or more. Leonard froze when he saw me. The other man walked up to me, reaching out his hand. "I'm Bryce."

I took his hand. "Nice to meet you."

Leonard just stood in the doorway, paralyzed, gaping at me like Death had come to his door. "What are you doing here?"

"It's good to see you too, Len," I replied.

"Destroying my career wasn't enough for you? You had to come and gloat?"

The conversation would have been awkward under any circumstances, but in front of my new colleagues it was painful. "Can we discuss this in private?"

"Kicking me to the curb wasn't private."

"I didn't kick you to the curb, Len. I had nothing to do with your being transferred."

"Then it was just sheer coincidence that I was fired a week after you arrived at LB?"

"Like you said, Potts likes to make human sacrifices."

"Back off, Lenny," Bryce said. "He's one of us now."

The way he said that sounded ominous. "One of us?" I asked.

"The outcasts. The Leo Burnett untouchables."

I glanced over at Charlene. She nodded sadly.

"Welcome to the eastern front," Bryce said. "You had to do something to get sent here. Offend a client. Put the wrong discount on a coupon. Heck, use the wrong deodorant. Usually it's nothing skill-related or they'd just fire you. Instead they send you here and hope you'll quit."

Charlene said, "There are no secrets in Siberia, Joseph. So what did you do?"

"What did *you* do?" I asked.

"I used to be Mr. Ferrell's personal assistant," Charlene said.

"Mr. Ferrell?" I said. She looked surprised that I didn't know who that was. "Mr. Ferrell is the CEO of Leo Burnett New York."

"I should have known that," I said. "So what did you do?"

"I made a derogatory comment about the CEO of Nintendo."

"That's it?"

"Unfortunately, Mr. Satou was standing behind me."

"Oh," I said.

I looked at Bryce. "And what's your story?"

"Love triangle. Copy chief and I both had our eye on the same woman. She chose me, so I got demoted back to junior and sent here. Lost my desk and the girl. But it's temporary, that rat won't be there forever."

"And the girl?"

"That's permanent. She showed her colors."

"We all know Lenny's story," Charlene said, making a face. "We've only heard it a few million times."

"It bears repetition," Leonard said.

Bryce nodded. "I'll abridge it. Some upstart, ambitious whiz kid came to Chicago and pushed him out."

Leonard's eyes narrowed at me.

"Good fiction," I said.

Leonard's expression grew more intense.

"I had nothing to do with it," I said.

"What's your story?" Bryce asked.

"Do tell," Leonard said fiercely.

I shook my head. "Like you, my offense wasn't skill-related. My manager's fiancée hit on me. He caught her on me at the company Christmas party. She blamed it on me of course."

"Yikes," Bryce said.

"That would do it," Charlene said. "He couldn't fire you because you'd win a wrongful termination suit, so he makes you want to quit."

Leonard looked at me with a satisfied expression. "So you and Brandi mixed it up."

"We didn't mix anything," I said. "The woman wouldn't leave me alone."

"I don't blame her," Charlene said. "You're hotter than a New York summer brown-out."

"That's sexual harassment," Bryce said.

"Sue me," Charlene said.

"So how does it work here?" I asked.

"I'm the office manager," Charlene said. "The main office sends me their copy requests, I deliver them to you, you write them and I send them back to a senior creative who checks your work then passes it on."

"It's humiliating," Bryce said. "I was a senior creative."

"If they disapprove," Charlene continued, "they'll send it

back with suggestions. I already have a half-dozen assign-
ments waiting for you."

"Okay," I said. "Where do I work?"

"Over there. You're in the office next to Leonard."

"Karma stinks, doesn't it, J.J.?" Leonard said.

"Whatever, man," I said. "Whatever."

# CHAPTER

## Twenty-three

*There are dreams that are meant to be shared
and dreams to be kept hidden in our hearts.
It's sometimes difficult to know which is which.*

✦ Joseph Jacobson's Diary ✦

Even though Leonard continued to detest me, the L.B. OutᴴKasts, as Bryce called us (he inverted the *K* to look Siberian, or, at least, Russian), were a close-knit group. We ate lunch together every day—usually takeout from a very good Thai restaurant across Seventh Avenue. We also played cards. Charlene was big on Hearts, so we played almost every day.

Truthfully, the sink tank wasn't bad duty. We left for home on time and rarely heard from the mother ship. I grew rather fond of Charlene and took to calling her Charbaby, which was politically incorrect on many levels, but made her smile every time.

One day we were playing cards at lunch when Charlene said, "What's this?" She was rifling through a file I had carried into our lunchroom.

"Nothing. Just some things I've been playing around with. I don't want to get rusty, so sometimes I create campaigns on my own."

"Mind if I look through them?"

"Knock yourself out."

She slowly flipped through the file, reading everything. A few times she burst out laughing. "These are terrific," she said.

"They're okay," I replied.

"Okay? Some of these are brilliant. In my career I've seen scores of writers come and go, and I know talent. If I ever get back with Mr. Ferrell, I'm going to tell him about you."

I just smiled at her. "I'm sure you will."

She was bothered that I had taken what she said so lightly. "I'm not just saying that, J.J. Can I take some of these?"

"Take them all," I said.

"Okay." She slid the file under her arm. "You'll see."

"I can't wait," I said, turning back to my cards. "Now who has the queen?"

"Speaking of queens," Leonard said. "Did I ever tell you that J.J. is a dreamer? He claims he sees the future in his dreams."

"I don't get the segue," Bryce said.

I looked at Leonard and shook my head. "Leave it alone, Len."

"It's true," Leonard said. "That's how he came up with the BankOne Bank On It campaign. He dreamt it even before he knew we needed it."

"That was yours?" Bryce asked. "That was a great campaign."

"You can tell the future?" Charlene asked.

"No. I mean, sometimes I dream things and they come true."

"I believe in dreams," Charlene said. "When I was ten, my mother had a dream that she was feeding my little brother bread. The next day he swallowed a bottle of cleaning solvent. Instead of making him throw up, she fed him bread. It saved his life."

"How many of your dreams come true?" Bryce asked.

"Most of them," I said.

"What kind of dreams do you have?" Charlene asked.

"All kinds. The other night I had a dream about the three of you."

"Tell us," Charlene said.

I looked into their eager faces. "Let's just play cards."

"You can't tell us you've seen our future then go on playing cards," Bryce said.

"I didn't say I had seen your future. I just had a dream about you."

"Am I going to die?" Bryce asked.

"C'mon, guys," I said. "Let's play."

"I knew it," Bryce said. "I'm dying."

"We're probably all dying," Leonard said.

"My dream wasn't about anyone dying," I said. "Come on, let's play cards."

"No, I have to know about your dream," Charlene said.

All three of them had stopped playing cards and were looking at me.

"C'mon," Leonard said. "Tell us what it was about."

"All right," I finally said. "But I'm not claiming to know the future."

"Have you ever been wrong?" Bryce asked.

I hesitated. "There are a few dreams that haven't come true."

"A few?"

"Two."

"Out of how many?"

I took a slow, deep breath. "Hundreds."

"Great," Leonard said.

"That's precisely why I don't want to tell you," I said.

"If it was something good, he would have already told us," Leonard said.

"We won't hold you to it," Bryce said. "Just tell us. Inquiring minds want to know."

I looked at them. There was no way they were going to drop it.

"All right. But don't say I didn't warn you."

"I know I'm going to die in it," Bryce said.

I ignored his comment. "My dream took place right here," I said. "I was sitting at my desk when you all came to me carrying small, robin's-egg blue boxes."

"Like Tiffany," Bryce said.

"Right," I said.

"I love Tiffany," Charlene said. "This is a good dream."

"All three of you asked me to tell you your future," I said.

"Just like we are now," Charlene said. "It's already coming true. Go on."

"I said to you, 'Let me see your boxes.' Charlene, you went first. You handed me your box and I lifted its lid. Inside was a miniature day planner. I said, 'You will soon return to being Mr. Ferrell's personal assistant.'"

Charlene leaned across the table hugged me. "Thank you. Thank you."

"It's just a dream," I said.

"It's a good dream," she replied.

"What about me?" Bryce said.

"You were next. I opened your box. Inside was a pen with an ink refill. I said, 'You'll soon return to the agency as a senior copywriter.' "

Bryce pumped his fist. "Yes! Does Scott die?"

"I didn't dream about Scott," I said.

"It would be an even better dream if Scott died in a fiery car crash," Bryce said.

Leonard looked at me. "What was in my box?"

I grimaced. "It's kind of strange."

"What was it," Leonard asked.

"It's a dream, okay? It doesn't matter what was in your box."

"It was something bad, wasn't it? Like a rattlesnake or grenade or something."

"No, there wasn't a snake. And it doesn't matter."

"You're right, it doesn't matter. So tell me."

"Fine," I said. "I opened your box and it had broken pots."

"Pots?"

"Yes. Little earthenware pots."

"What does that mean?"

"I'm not sure," I said.

Leonard looked frantic. "You're not *sure*? You knew what theirs meant."

"I'm sorry. I don't know."

"If the pots are broken, it's got to be bad," Charlene said.

"Maybe it means that you won't be able to hold anything," Bryce said. "Like money, or a relationship."

". . . Or a job," Charlene said.

Leonard looked even more distressed. "This is stupid. It's just a dream."

"That's what I said."

Leonard shook his head. "You still have it out for me."

"I've never had it out for you," I said. "It's just a dream."

"More like a nightmare," he replied.

I got up. "Okay, I'm done. I'm going back to work."

As I walked out, I heard Leonard say, "It's a stupid dream. It doesn't mean a thing."

# CHAPTER

## *Twenty-four*

*My winter has too soon been followed by another.*

✦ Joseph Jacobson's Diary ✦

Two days later it was my turn to pick up lunch. I went up front to get Charlene's order, but she wasn't there. I found Leonard and Bryce in the conference room.

"Hey, where's Char?" I asked.

"I think she's sick," Leonard said.

"No," Bryce said. "She called in this morning and said she'd be in late. Something about a meeting."

"I bet she's job-hunting," Leonard said.

"Could you blame her?" Bryce said. "She's got too much light to be kept under a bushel."

The thought of her leaving the tank made me sad. "That's too bad," I said. "Not for her but for us."

Even Leonard nodded in agreement. "I was thinking of asking her out."

Bryce and I glanced at each other but said nothing.

An hour after lunch my phone rang. "Joseph, it's Charlene."

"Charbaby," I said. "What's going on? We missed you at lunch. We had to listen to Leonard tell us about his date last week."

"I'm so sorry," she said.

"I don't think he had a date. I'm pretty sure he's just recycling old ones. Or someone else's."

"Did the date pull out a hair and floss her teeth with it?"

"How did you know that?"

"Disney Channel," she said. "Listen, I have some news."

"What's up?"

"I just got my job back as Mr. Ferrell's personal assistant."

"That's fantastic."

"Just like you saw in your dream. On my way in to work this morning, Mr. Ferrell called and asked me to come see him. He said his new assistant is driving him crazy and he wants me back."

"Congratulations. I'm so happy for you. Not so much for us, but definitely for you."

"Thanks. I'll miss you too."

Bryce walked up, leaning over my desk. "What's up with Char?"

"What's going on?" Leonard asked.

"Bryce and Leonard want to know. Can I tell them?"

"Tell us what?" Bryce asked.

"Go ahead," Charlene said.

I put the phone on speaker. "You tell them. You're on speaker, go ahead."

"I got my job back," Charlene said.

"Yes!" Bryce shouted. "I knew you would. Just like J.J.'s dream. Now I'm next."

"The dream is bogus," Leonard said.

"We're really happy for you," I said again.

"Make that a double," Bryce said.

"Thank you. But I'm going to miss working with you all. I hate breaking up the OutKasts."

"We can still get together for Hearts," I said. "Besides, you never belonged here."

"None of us belong there," she said. "Except Leonard."

"How you mock me," Leonard said.

"Joseph, would it be too much trouble to have you bring my things from my desk over to my new office? There's not that much and the last assistant left things such a mess that I won't be able to get out of here for at least a week."

"Sure. No problem. What floor?"

"I'm on the eighteenth floor. If I'm not there, just leave the box at my desk."

"You'll have it before the day's out."

"I owe you," she said. "When things let up, let's all get together for lunch."

"And Hearts," Bryce added.

"Of course. I better go. Mr. Ferrell just finished his call."

"Congratulations again," I said.

"Oh, Joseph," she said.

"Yes?"

"Don't stop dreaming."

# CHAPTER

## *Twenty-five*

*We speak hopefully of the Phoenix rising from ashes, but forget that the fire was of the Phoenix's own making.*

✦ Joseph Jacobson's Diary ✦

It was a lot quieter around the office without Charlene. Based on seniority, Leonard was promoted to office manager, which was a little frightening. Never in the recorded history of humanity had so little power gone to someone's head. Still, Bryce and I pretty much ignored most of what he said.

Days crawled and the months flew. Summer passed. Then fall. I saw a news story about a polygamist leader in southern Utah being arrested, and I wondered about April. I missed her. I had missed Ashley, but now, in retrospect, I felt as if I'd dodged a bullet. With April, I felt nothing but regret. I was lonely. My money was dwindling. And there was nothing to look for on the horizon. It seemed to me that everyone's ships had sailed but mine.

Two months later Bryce came running into my office.

"It happened! J.J., it happened!"

I looked up from my computer. "What happened?"

"They're bringing me back. Benefits, salary, the whole package. And, bonus, Scott is getting the boot. There is a God in Heaven and He is smiling on me."

Leonard walked up behind him, holding a half-eaten bagel. "You got your job back?"

"Just like J.J. dreamed," Bryce said. He turned back to me. "You, my friend, have a gift."

I was happy for him, but sad for me. At least I was better at hiding it than Leonard, who looked like he'd just been diagnosed with cancer.

"Congratulations," I said. "When do you leave?"

"The train is at the station," he said. "After lunch."

"Just don't forget your friends out here in Siberia."

"Never." He turned to Leonard. "Still think J.J.'s dreams are bogus?"

Leonard didn't answer. I thought he might throw up.

We shared a celebratory lunch, then sent Bryce and his things off to Park Avenue South in a taxi. Leonard moped around the rest of the afternoon. Just before quitting time he came into my office and collapsed into a chair, his legs spread, his head down. "When does the ax fall?"

I looked up from the coupon I was writing. "What ax?"

"The one over my neck."

"It was just a dream. You said so yourself."

"You don't really believe that," he said.

"What does it matter what I believe? It's your life. Besides, all I saw was broken pots. I have no idea what it means. Neither do you."

"I know what it means," he said. "Dead man walking."

I sighed. "Sorry, man. I didn't want to tell you."

"You shouldn't have," he said. "You should keep things like that to yourself."

"Yeah, I tried that."

He looked down at the floor for a minute, then said,

"There's a news station in Reno that needs a copywriter. I put in an application." He got up and walked out of my office.

Winter settled in, chilling the city to its concrete bones. I felt as dismal as the gray skies that hovered over the island. I supposed I was losing hope. Charlene and Bryce had got out, returning to where they started—something that wasn't going to happen to Leonard or me. Chicago was barred and a promotion in New York seemed impossible. Career advancement is unlikely when you're invisible, and that's what I was. Invisible. I felt as if the world had forgotten I existed.

I considered looking for a new job, but in a market as competitive as New York, that would require superhuman energy, confidence and references. I had none of the above.

Part of me still fantasized about returning to Colorado, back to the days of blissful ignorance—secure in the false belief that my family loved me and that Ashley and I were meant for each other. It was a pleasant fiction but still a lie. And you can't squeeze happiness from an exposed lie any more than you can drink real water from a mirage.

Most of all, I missed April. Sometimes so much that my chest ached. I missed her and hated myself for not loving her the way she had loved me. In my banishment from Colorado, I had chosen to pay for someone else's sin. But in my banishment from April, the sin was mine. And that made the pain much, much worse. I had no idea how I could ever get her back.

There was nothing left to do but resign myself to Fate, hoping that she might have some mercy left for me—and that my heart didn't give out before it came.

✦

When you work with just one person, you either like them, learn to tolerate them, or kill them. Odd as it may sound, the better I got to know Leonard, the more I liked him. He kind of grew on me. Like mold.

In spite of his DayGlo insecurity and complete lack of social skills, he had a good heart. He wasn't really a bad writer either, though he was inconsistent. Every now and then, Leonard would come up with something surprisingly brilliant, reminding me why he had been hired in the first place. He probably struck out more times than he knocked it out of the park, but so did Babe Ruth.

On Thursday, November 17, I was working on a direct-mail piece for HoneyBaked Hams when the phone rang. It was still just Leonard and me, and Leonard had assigned me the task of answering the phone.

"Leo Burnett," I said.

"Joseph, it's Charlene."

"Charbaby," I said.

"That's so un-PC," she said. "Never stop."

"Promise. It's so good to hear your voice. So how's life at the top?"

"Why don't you come find out for yourself?"

"I'd be happy to," I said flippantly. "Just show me the way."

"I can do more than that. I can open the door for you. Mr. Ferrell would like to meet with you."

"What?"

"You heard me. Mr. Ferrell would like to meet you. He asked me to call you to make an appointment."

I couldn't think of any reason why the president and CEO of Leo Burnett New York would want to talk to me. "Why?"

"Remember those ads of yours I took?"

"Yes."

"I gave them to Mr. Ferrell to look at. He was seriously impressed. I told you they were good. So catch a cab and get right over here."

"I'll be right there," I said.

"I can't wait to see you again," Charlene said. "You dream boy."

Ten minutes later I stepped out of the elevator on the eighteenth floor into the executive suite. Charlene smiled when she saw me. She pushed a button on her phone. "He's here, sir."

A deep male voice boomed, "Send him in."

She stood up from her desk and we embraced. "Are you ready?"

"I'm not sure what I'm supposed to be ready for."

"To dream." She opened the door to Mr. Ferrell's office, putting her hand on the small of my back as I walked in.

Mr. George Ferrell was a tall, well-groomed man, dressed in an ash gray Valentino suit, with French cuffs and gold cufflinks peeking out beneath the coat sleeves. He had a full head of hair, which was impeccably coiffed and lightly peppered with gray. He was fit, tan and confident-looking. Everything about him, including his office, seemed to exude energy.

"Joseph," he said, eyeing me as I entered. "Come in, come in."

I walked up to his desk.

"Sit down," he said.

"Yes, sir." I sat.

He looked me over until I began to feel self-conscious. "I've had the chance to look over more than twenty campaigns you've written. Are they all yours?"

"Yes, sir."

He nodded. "You're very talented," he said. "Charlene tells me that we've had you rotting over in the satellite office. How did that come about?"

"You want the whole story?"

"Condense it," he said. "Isn't that what we admen do best—package long stories into bite-sized nuggets."

"Fair enough. I was hired at Leo Burnett Chicago from a small Colorado agency. My first week there I came up with a campaign for BankOne which landed me a promotion as creative head of the BankOne team."

"That wouldn't be the Bank On It, campaign?"

"Yes, sir."

He nodded. "I used it as an example of excellence in one of our board meetings. Continue."

"Things were going well until I ran afoul of our creative director, Peter Potts."

"What happened?"

"His fiancée wanted to get to know me better."

"Not good."

"No, sir. Because it was a personal matter, Potts couldn't fire me, so he demoted me and sent me as far away as he could—the New York satellite office. That's pretty much it."

He thought over my story for a moment, then said, "Okay, now let's leave that all behind. You're very good at what you do, Joseph. Your ideas are fresh and memorable. On our rating scale these are seven plus. Some of them border on genius."

He stood, walking to the side of his desk. "Leo Burnett said, 'I have learned that any fool can write a bad ad, but that it takes a real genius to keep his hands off a good one.'

"Unfortunately, we have a shortage of geniuses. In today's advertising environment, no one can keep their hands to themselves.

"The quality of today's advertising is in decline. There was a time when admen were as revered as poets and statesmen. In the fifties, more people watched the television commercials than the programs. Can you imagine that? In the sixties, the David Ogilvy days, Alka-Seltzer ads became America's catchphrases.

"I believe that we've lost our way, not because admen are getting less creative, but because they're becoming more cautious—and that's because our clients are becoming more cautious. On the surface this might sound like a good thing, but it's not. Caution never breeds greatness. Caution is the birthplace of mediocrity.

"Look at the movie industry. Indies aside, all Hollywood produces these days are prequels, sequels and comic books. Will we ever have another *Casablanca* or *Citizen Kane?* I doubt it.

"The reality is that the more people there are who have to sign off on a campaign, the more diluted and weaker the campaign becomes. All great ideas, every revolution, started as a spark, not in a boardroom, but in one man or woman's mind.

"This worldwide agency was built by one man with big ideas. Leo Burnett created icons the world embraced for generations. And as a reward for their trust, his clients made billions. Could you imagine trying to pass the Jolly Green Giant through one of today's marketing committees? It would never happen.

"Today, creative ideas are being run through bureaucratic grinders until everything is pablum."

"Pablum?"

"Mush," he said. "Flavorless, bland and pasty. I want to see if we can counter that trend. I've been looking for the right talent to wrestle Creative back from the committee mentality. I think that someone is you."

I looked at him in disbelief. "Me?"

"I didn't just see those campaigns of yours today. I've been studying them for weeks. I've shared them with the people I trust most. There's a raw brilliance to them, maybe more than you know."

"I'm flattered, really, but I don't have much experience with the business side of advertising."

"Exactly," he said, pointing at me. "I want someone unblemished by the internal systems we've created that have fostered this decline.

"I have a dream of a creative renaissance starting right here at Leo Burnett. I want you to champion our creative teams as the direct liaison with our clients. I want to weaken the committee syndrome and bring about a new golden age for advertising. I want you to encourage our creative teams to do what they do best—create. I want you to find where and how we are punishing our innovators and remedy that. This will be a new, unique position, answering only to me." He sat back against the edge of the desk. "So, what do you think?"

"About the concept or your offer?"

He smiled at my question. "Both."

"I believe you're right about the committee effect. I started my career in a small agency with mid-range regional clients. That gave us a lot more control and flexibility, which is why we were able to outperform our larger competition, both in awards and results."

Ferrell nodded. "My point exactly."

"As far as your offer, I hope your faith in me is not misplaced, but I'd be a fool to turn it down. When do we start?"

Ferrell smiled. "Right now," he said, walking to the front of his office. "Come over to the table, let me show you how we're going to realize my dream."

# CHAPTER

## *Twenty-six*

*I have wondered why it is that our greatest triumphs
spring from our greatest extremity and adversity. Perhaps
it is because we are so resistant to change, we only
move when our seat becomes too hot to occupy.*

✴ Joseph Jacobson's Diary ✴

Mr. Ferrell named his program The Florence Initiative (TFI), in homage to Florence, Italy, the birthplace of the Renaissance. The tranquil nine-to-five days of the satellite office were long gone. Everything happened so fast that I didn't even get the chance to see Leonard to say goodbye, though I did call him. To my surprise he sounded genuinely happy with my promotion. I was glad I had gotten to know him.

I was given an office next to Mr. Ferrell's, with a beautiful view of Seventh Avenue. I hired my own personal assistant—Krysten—a young marketing graduate from Nebraska. My salary more than quadrupled. I was given a starting bonus, an extravagant wardrobe allowance, an expense account and a gym membership at the New York Athletic Club. I'm not saying my personal life was great, but suffering in luxury is still better than suffering in poverty.

Backed by Mr. Ferrell's passion, our TFI program hit the agency like a flash flood. I spent the next six months meeting with each of the Leo Burnett New York creative teams and reviewing all of the campaigns the agency was working on—which meant hundreds of hours of reading, critiquing and follow-up. I didn't mind the long hours. For centuries, men and women have thrown themselves into their work to avoid confronting the pain of their own grief.

Mr. Ferrell was spot-on about the committee syndrome and its crippling effect on our creative work. Viewing the campaigns before and after committee approval was like seeing a boxer's face before and after the title fight. It was my job to champion the "before" and restore our Creative's original intent.

I didn't expect it to be easy and it wasn't. At first the creative directors were suspicious of my motives and threatened by my involvement with their work. But, as I showed them that my goal was to put them back in charge of their own ideas, they changed their tune. In fact, I was soon seen as their greatest ally. One of them even coined a title for me, which was quickly adopted agency-wide: Creative Czar.

It took nearly a year for Mr. Ferrell's vision to pay off. But it did. As our Creative started generating buzz on Madison Avenue, Wall Street, and Main Street America, our clients began putting more power back in our hands.

*Ad Age* magazine ran a front-page feature on the new face of Leo Burnett, actually using the headline "Agency Renaissance." There was only one mention of me in the article and they got my name wrong, John Jacobson, but I didn't care. It made Mr. Ferrell look good, and making your boss look good is good for job security.

Besides, the idea was his, not mine. What Mr. Ferrell had dreamed about, a creative renaissance, was actually coming true. With all the success and accolades, I shouldn't have been surprised when, with the holidays approaching, everything changed.

# CHAPTER

## Twenty-seven

*Things are going well, which, of course, means it's time for change.*
*Fate abhors nothing so much as contentment.*

✦ Joseph Jacobson's Diary ✦

The day before Thanksgiving, Charlene buzzed me in my office. "J.J., Mr. Ferrell would like to meet with you."

"Right now?"

"Yes. Immediately."

"Tell him I'll be right in."

Charlene smiled as I approached her desk. "He's waiting."

"Thanks."

Mr. Ferrell was sitting at his desk. In front of him was a bottle of Dom Perignon and two long-stemmed crystal champagne glasses.

"What can I do for you, sir?" I asked.

"Have a seat, Joe." (Mr. Ferrell was the only one at the firm who I allowed to call me Joe. He told me to call him George, but I never felt comfortable with it.) I sat down in the leather chair facing his desk.

"Are you ready for Thanksgiving?" he asked.

"Yes, it's easy. I'm spending it alone."

"Sounds refreshingly simple. We've got all of Peggy's family coming over. Maybe I'll join you."

"Let me know," I said. "I'll pick up another Hungry-Man frozen dinner."

He smiled, then his demeanor turned more serious. "I need to tell you something." He leaned back in his chair. "Last night I received a phone call from Don Shelton. Do you know who that is?"

"No, sir."

"Don's the Chairman of the Board for Leo Burnett. He gave me some news that I'd like to share with you."

"Yes, sir."

"First the good news. The rumors you've heard milling about the energy rooms are true. I've been promoted to CEO of Leo Burnett Worldwide."

"That's fantastic news," I said. "You deserve it."

"Thank you," he said, downplaying my excitement. "Now the bad news."

My excitement drained nearly as fast as it had come. I looked at him anxiously.

"With me leaving, I'm afraid there won't be a place for you here in the New York office."

I fought back my disappointment and surprise. "I'm sorry to hear that. I thought things were going well."

"And they have been," he said. "But if business has taught me anything, it's that nothing is as constant as change." He looked at me for a moment, then said, "I hope losing your job here doesn't stifle your creative flow, because I'd like you to come with me as the new Global Chief Creative Officer for Leo Burnett Worldwide."

I stared at him in disbelief. "You're promoting me?"

Grinning, he opened the bottle of champagne and poured it into the glasses on his desk. "Of course I am." He lifted both glasses and then walked around the desk to the front, offering one of the glasses to me. "You'll be my number one."

I was speechless.

"We work well together," Mr. Ferrell said. "I'm no fool. The Florence Initiative is the main reason I got the promotion. And we've just begun. I believe that the two of us can fulfill my dream of a creative renaissance—not just for Leo Burnett, but for the whole world."

"I believe so too, sir."

"I know. You're a dreamer like me."

I held up my glass. "To the dream."

"No," Mr. Ferrell said, holding up his glass. "To the dreamers."

# CHAPTER

## Twenty-eight

*Life has granted me the most operatic of circumstances.*

✦ Joseph Jacobson's Diary ✦

Mr. Ferrell's and my promotions meant we'd be moving to the Leo Burnett international headquarters in Chicago. Chicago. I was apprehensive about returning, though I admit I was looking forward to seeing the look on Potts's face when I walked back in as his boss's boss's boss. *Definitely worth the flight.*

It would not be so gratifying to confront my memories of April. I decided that rather than ignore my pain, when I got back to Chicago, I would go back to the diner and put my memories to rest.

At any rate, Mr. Ferrell wouldn't be moving to Chicago for about three weeks, allowing enough time for him to hand over the reins of the New York agency to his successor. I planned to leave New York around the same time Mr. Ferrell did. In the meantime, there was a lot to do to prepare for the change.

Two weeks into our transition, Mr. Ferrell called me into his office.

"Joe, didn't you say you're from the Rocky Mountain area?"

"Colorado," I said.

"Colorado. Perfect. We need a presence in the Rocky

Mountain area and we've been looking at purchasing an existing agency in Utah or Colorado. There's a Colorado agency that looks especially promising. In fact, it looks prime for the plucking." He handed me a file. "Are you familiar with this agency?"

I looked at the sheet. My heart froze.

## Jacobson Advertising and Public Relations
### 2001 Altura Drive, Denver, Colorado

"Yes, sir."

"What do you know about it?"

"Just about everything," I said. "That's where I started. I worked there for eight years."

Mr. Ferrell looked pleased with this revelation. "Interesting firm, Jacobson. Over the last fifteen years they've won practically every award possible. They used to have a stellar reputation, but over the last year their stock has plummeted.

"Our executive management team looked into it. As you know it's a family-run business. The CEO is the father, Israel Jacobson. He's been rather ill for the last year. With the downturn in the economy and his absence, they've lost their three largest accounts. If someone doesn't save them soon, the business may go under. I'd like you to investigate the firm and see if it's worth saving. Can you handle this for me?"

The news about my father being ill left me reeling. "I'll do whatever you want, sir. But I should disclose that I have a conflict of interest."

"Tell me about it."

"Our parting was less than amicable. They forced me out of the agency."

"No doubt one of their greatest faux pas on their way to decline," Mr. Ferrell said.

"I'm not sure I can be totally objective."

"You'll be better than objective. You'll be passionate."

"The agency is owned by my family."

Mr. Ferrell raised an eyebrow. "You weren't kidding when you said you know the agency, were you?"

"No, sir."

"Still, if it's not too difficult, I'd like you to handle it. I have complete confidence in you. Will you do this for me?"

"Absolutely."

"Very well. I'll look forward to your report."

On the way back to my office I stopped at my assistant's desk, handing her the paper Mr. Ferrell had given me. "Krysten, I need you to contact Rupert and Simon Jacobson at this firm. They know who we are. Tell them I'd like to meet with them in our offices this Thursday afternoon."

She looked at the paper. "Jacobson Advertising." She looked up at me. "Jacobson. Any relation?"

"Distant," I replied. "Very distant."

"All right," she said. "How long would you like me to schedule the meeting for?"

"Keep my entire afternoon open. It may go long." I started to walk away, then stopped and turned back. "Krysten, one more thing. Don't tell them my last name. Just call me Mr. Joseph."

She looked at me quizzically. "Why is that?"

"Simple," I said. "I don't want them to know who I am."

# CHAPTER

# *Twenty-nine*

*Even a broken heart can still hold love.*

✦ Joseph Jacobson's Diary ✦

I hardly slept Wednesday night. My emotions ranged wildly. My brothers had sent me out into the wilderness. I should have hated them for what they did, but if they hadn't banished me, I never would have achieved what I had. I never would have become creative director of one of the world's largest advertising agencies. Nor would I have met April. Considering how much I had suffered over losing her, that may not seem like a good thing. But even as painful as our separation was, I still would have chosen to meet her. To have felt her love, even for the short time I had it, was better than to not know that such love existed. At least that's what I told myself.

No matter my brothers' intent, no matter the pain they'd inflicted on me, I was grateful for what they had done. But that had little to do with the purchasing of the advertising agency. The bigger question was, could I work with them? And that depended on the biggest question of all: Given the chance, would they do what they had done again? Had they remorse for sending me away? That was what would determine whether or not we could work together.

Ultimately, their hearts would determine their fates.

Thursday morning, as I was shaving, I took a good look at myself in the bathroom mirror. I had changed a lot in the last three years. Not just mentally and emotionally, but physically as well. I inventoried those changes. I had lost weight and grown more muscular. More angular. I had changed my hairstyle, which was a much bigger thing than you might expect. My father, being a soldier during the "make love not war" sixties, abhorred "hippie hair." So, like my brothers, I had always kept it short and above the ear. Now it touched my collar and my ears were all but invisible. My father would be aghast.

My wardrobe had changed dramatically as well—thanks to a change of scene and a company credit card. I definitely looked more suited to New York than Denver. Getting ready for work, I put on a navy blue Armani suit with a turtleneck. I doubted they'd recognize me. Honestly, I don't think I would have recognized me.

There were also the intangibles. I once read somewhere that context is 90 percent of recognition, and my brothers certainly weren't expecting to see me. Still, if you've ever read a romance novel, you know the eyes are always the giveaway.

I put on a pair of yellow-lens Ray-Ban sunglasses, then took out my Colorado driver's license and compared visages in the mirror. A cop would definitely question my identity. I was certain that my brothers wouldn't recognize me.

As I walked into my office, I reminded Krysten not to use my real name. An hour later she buzzed my office.

"They're here," she said.

My heart raced. "Show them in."

"Right away."

Rupert came in first. While I had worried about him recognizing me, the truth was, I almost didn't recognize him. Actually either of them. Simon had also changed. They looked older: gray and weary, the way stress and hard times change you.

"Mr. Joseph," Rupert said, extending his hand. "I'm Rupert Jacobson. It's a pleasure meeting you."

I stood, firmly taking his hand. "It's my pleasure." I turned to Simon, thinking he had changed even more than Rupert. "And you are?"

"Simon Jacobson," he said, extending his hand.

I took his hand. The same hand that had given me the pen to sign my resignation. "Jacobsons. Are you brothers?"

"Yes, sir," Simon said.

"So it's a family business. Have a seat."

After they were seated, Rupert said, "You have a beautiful office."

"Thank you," I said. "You should see the skyline at night. Last week the Empire State Building was lit green and black to celebrate the twenty-year anniversary of *Wicked*." I sat down at my desk and leaned back in my chair, studying them. I wondered if, on a subconscious level, they recognized my voice. "You must forgive my glasses. I've just had my eyes examined. They're dilated."

"Of course," Rupert said, smiling nervously. "I just thought you looked cool. Like Bono."

Simon likewise smiled. "Me too," he said.

"As you know," I said, "Leo Burnett is looking at expanding into the Rocky Mountain area and we're interested in your firm. We've examined your books, but I'd like to hear about your agency from you." I turned to Rupert. "You're the CEO?"

"No, sir. I'm the general manager."

"Oh," I said, feigning disappointment. "This meeting wasn't important enough for your CEO?"

Rupert blanched. "No, sir," he said quickly. "I mean, it was, sir. It's just that our CEO hasn't been well lately. He hasn't been able to travel."

Even though Mr. Ferrell had told me this earlier, hearing it from my brothers made it somehow more real. I took a moment to compose myself. "Your CEO isn't well?"

"No, sir."

I hesitated, gathering my emotions. "What's wrong with him?"

"You might say we've suffered a loss in the family," he said. "He's not dealing with it very well."

This news frightened me. I wondered about my mother and Ben. What if something had happened to one of them? I struggled to remain stoic. "Has there been a death?"

"No," Rupert said. "One of his sons left home. He took it very hard."

"I'm sorry to hear that," I said softly. "Losing a family member can be difficult. How about you two? It must have been difficult for you as well."

They were both quiet.

"No?"

"It's been very difficult," Rupert said.

I eyed Simon. "Was it?"

He nodded.

"What is his name? This brother of yours."

Simon looked uncomfortable. "I'm not sure that this discussion is relevant to . . ."

"Normally it wouldn't be," I said sternly. "But since we're looking at purchasing a family business, I would think the state of the family would be extremely relevant to our investigation, wouldn't you, Mr. Jacobson?"

He squirmed uncomfortably in his seat. "Yes, sir. My apologies. I just didn't want to get too personal."

"The nature of this investment is personal. What is your brother's name?"

"It's Joseph, sir," Simon said.

"And why did he leave?"

Long silence. Then Simon said, "He wanted to try something new—a bigger agency. In fact, he was hired by your agency. Leo Burnett of Chicago."

"Then he's with us," I said. "Interesting. I assume he's still employed there."

"We're not sure," Rupert said. "We've lost contact with him."

"I can check on that. Since he understands the Leo Burnett corporate culture, I'm sure that what he'd have to tell us about the compatibility of our two agencies will be helpful."

Both of the men looked anxious.

I turned to Simon. "If I ask him why he left, he'll corroborate your story?"

More silence. Then Simon said, "No, sir. He probably won't."

"What would he tell me?"

"He would probably say that it was my fault he left. I forced him out."

I frowned. "Why would you do that?"

Another pause.

"This is very uncomfortable."

"Please continue. The more I know, the better prepared I will be to make a recommendation to our CEO."

Simon exhaled slowly. "I was jealous of him. He was more talented than me and my father knew it. I was afraid I would lose my job to him."

I looked at him coolly. "This concerns me," I said. "A corporate culture that punishes success will never succeed."

"Clearly," Rupert said.

"Have you sought to make amends with this brother?"

"We've wanted to," Rupert said. I noticed the emotion in his eyes. "But we didn't know how to reach him."

"You just told me he was employed with our Chicago office. Certainly you could have found him."

"The truth is," Simon said, "we were too ashamed."

Rupert nodded in agreement.

After a moment I exhaled slowly. "Okay. Enough of this

matter." I lifted a sheet of paper. "We had our accounting department conduct a detailed audit of the last five years of your financial books. They've brought something to my attention. There seems to be a discrepancy in your finances.

"About three years ago there was a sizable nonitemized disbursement to one of your employees. If my memory doesn't fail me, his name is Benjamin."

I noticed both of them squirm.

"This Benjamin also has the last name of Jacobson so may I assume he's one of your family?"

"Yes, sir," the brothers said almost in unison.

"He's our brother," Rupert said.

"Another brother? How many of you are there?"

"Twelve brothers, sir," Simon said. "And one sister."

"What a family," I said, shaking my head as if in amazement. "But back to the company. The amount of the disbursement was thirty-six thousand dollars. What can you tell me about this?"

"He borrowed the money," Rupert said.

"Borrowed from a public held company?"

"Yes, sir."

"Are you a bank as well as an agency?"

"No, sir," Rupert said.

"I don't need to tell you that's not good business practice. But, why then wasn't this disbursement originally recorded as a loan? In fact, it would appear that there was an attempt to conceal it."

Both brothers sat silently.

"Is this something that your father was involved with?"

"No, sir," Rupert blurted out.

"Then your father, CEO, was unaware of what was going on at his own firm."

Rupert looked down for a moment, then back to me. "Mr. Joseph, I know this looks bad. But it's not my father's fault. This whole thing was a fiasco, but it was a fluke—a one-time event. Please keep this in the context of decades of company success."

"Noted," I said. I sat back and looked at them for a moment. I honestly felt bad for them. For their desperation. "I noticed a strange coincidence here. The time of this 'loan' coincides with your brother Joseph's departure from the firm. Was he somehow involved in this matter?"

"Yes," Simon said.

His answer surprised me. "He was?"

"It's just that I used that incident to coerce him to leave the firm."

"How did you do that?"

"He wanted to just pay the money back for his brother. But I told him that if he didn't leave the state I would file legal action against Ben. Ben is his full brother."

"F-o-o-l or f-u-l-l brother?" I asked.

"The latter," Rupert said.

"So, this Joseph is guilty of attempting to conceal what may be considered a fraudulent act. And he is currently working at our agency. Unfortunately, I'll have to respond to that."

Both brothers blanched.

"Mr. Joseph," Rupert said, "the only thing my brother

Joseph is guilty of is mercy. He had nothing to do with any of this. We put him in a horrible position. If anyone should be fired, it's me. This is my failure. I never should have involved him in this affair." He paused with emotion. "Let him keep his job. Please don't punish him for my actions."

"Unfortunately, that is the way the world works," I said. "Right or wrong, others are always affected by our actions."

"Then I ask you to let me pay for my mistake."

Simon looked up. "Make that two of us. The entire thing was my idea."

I gazed at them for a long time, realizing that, in a way, their course had been worse than mine. I wondered how much guilt they had carried for the last three years.

"Does your father know the truth about why his son left?"

They both shook their heads.

"He was so upset," Rupert said. "We were afraid he would just dissolve the agency and throw us out of his life. We deserved that, but *he* didn't deserve that."

I thought over his words. "So let me get this straight. You're telling me that you're both willing to sacrifice your jobs for this brother Joseph?"

They were both quiet, then Rupert said, "If it comes to that. Yes, I am."

"And you?" I asked Simon.

He nodded sadly. "Yes, sir."

Their answers filled me with emotion. "So tell me," I said softly. "If your brother Joseph was right here in this room, right now, what would you say to him?"

Simon's voice broke with emotion. "I would ask his forgiveness."

"And you?" I asked Rupert.

He nodded, too emotional to speak. "The same."

"Do you think he should grant you forgiveness?"

Simon looked down, then said, "No. He shouldn't. But I would hope he would at least know how sorry we are."

I was having trouble hiding my own emotion. I let the moment linger a bit longer, then I said, "Everyone makes mistakes. The real question is, what have we learned from them." I pushed back from the desk. "The thing about buying an agency is that we're not buying bricks and mortar. We're buying an organization. A past and, hopefully, a future. Jacobson has been a winning team for nearly thirty years. And you two men may share in the blame of this unfortunate incident, but you also share the credit for a lot of good work. Most of all, you have learned a valuable lesson."

I turned away and lifted my glasses to wipe my eyes. Then I turned back to them.

"The thing about life that is most interesting to me, is how often good comes from evil. If you hadn't banished your brother, you probably would still be resenting him . . . and he wouldn't be here today to save you and the agency."

Both brothers looked at me quizzically.

"I don't understand," Rupert said.

I took off my sunglasses. "Rupert. Simon. It's me."

They still didn't recognize me.

". . . Your brother Joseph."

I saw the light of recognition come to Rupert's eyes. "Joseph?"

"You don't know your own brother?"

Rupert began to cry. "J.J."

Simon sat there, staring in disbelief.

I walked to the front of my desk. Rupert also stood and we embraced. Then I turned to Simon. He was afraid to look at me. Ashamed.

"This was all my fault," he said, shaking his head.

"Then I have you to thank as well," I replied.

"I'm so sorry."

"I know you are. You just proved it."

He stood and we embraced. Then he began to cry. Actually, he began to sob, perhaps the release of years of guilt and remorse. "How can you forgive us after what we did to you?"

"That's what family does, brother. Forgive. Besides, you did me a favor. My life never would have been this full if it wasn't for you." I stepped back from Simon and smiled at them both as tears welled up in my eyes. "It's so good to see you again. Now come on. I'll show you the town. We've got a few years to catch up on."

# CHAPTER

## *Thirty*

*Life relishes irony. Only in losing my home have I truly gained it.*

✦ Joseph Jacobson's Diary ✦

That evening I took my brothers to one of my favorite restaurants in the city, Keens Steakhouse. I shared with them all that had happened after I left Denver. Not surprisingly, they wanted to meet Leonard and beat up Potts.

My biggest surprise of the evening was learning that just five months after I left Colorado, Ashley had married Chuck Teran, the fifty-two-year-old owner of UpHill Down. In fact, she had convinced him to drop our agency—just before moving with him to Palm Springs. I was truly in my brothers' debt.

Rupert and Simon flew home the next morning. I made them promise not to tell my father about me. We would tell him together when I came out to close on the purchasing of the agency. I thought it would be best that way.

Ten days later, only a week before Christmas, I flew home to Denver. Seeing the snow-capped Rockies out my airplane window sent a rush through my body. I can't describe the happiness I felt to be home. Even the *Blue Mustang* didn't look quite so demonic.

An hour after my return, I met up with the rest of the brothers. Rupert and Simon had already told them about our reunion, but I sensed they didn't really believe them until they saw me with their own eyes. I hugged each of them. It really was good to be home again.

Rupert and Judd brought my father down to the agency under the auspices of meeting "Mr. Joseph." My hair was still long and I was wearing my New York wardrobe, but my father recognized me immediately.

"Joseph," he shouted. He rushed forward and threw his arms around me and kissed my face. "You've come home," he said. "My boy has come home."

"I've missed you," I said, tears running down my cheeks. "Every day I worried about you."

"Every minute I worried about you," he said. "Every single minute."

The brothers stood watching the reunion—silent, astonished and ashamed. When the climax of our reunion had died down some, Rupert and Simon stepped forward. I had never seen either of them so anxious. Rupert said, "Dad, it's time you finally knew the truth about what happened."

My father turned and looked at him. "I already know, son. I've known the whole time."

"You knew we sent him away?" Rupert asked.

My father nodded. "Yes."

"I don't understand," Simon said. "Then why didn't you send us away?"

My father grew emotional. His eyes welled up with tears and he struggled to speak. "Because I was also to blame for what happened. I was careless with your feelings, and that too is a sin. I had already lost one of my sons. I didn't want to lose any more of you."

Ben looked at him sorrowfully. "You knew what I did?"

My father turned to him. "Yes."

"Why didn't you punish me?"

"You needed to learn that others will be hurt by your actions. You haven't gambled since Joseph left, have you?"

"No, sir."

"You owe your brother a huge debt of gratitude."

"I know," Ben said. His eyes filled with tears. He threw his arms around me. "I won't let you down again. Ever."

"I know," I said. "I've missed you."

Ben put his head on my shoulder and wept. After a few moments we parted. I said to my father, "Do you think I could have my jacket back?"

My father smiled. "I've been saving it for this day. It's at home. But I think you'd better see your mother first."

# CHAPTER

## *Thirty-one*

*This month I've seen the fulfillment of two dreams.*

✦ Joseph Jacobson's Diary ✦

My reunion with my mother was beautiful. She had never believed the story she had been told about my disappearance. She knew something bad had happened to me—she just didn't know what. And she never stopped praying that I would return home. "This is the greatest day of my life," she said, kissing my face. "The absolute greatest."

I made her promise that she would not hold what had happened to me against my brothers. She promised, but begrudgingly. "That doesn't mean I trust them," she said. "That, they'll have to earn back."

I spent Christmas in Denver. As joyful as I was to be home, my heart was still hurting. Being so close to Utah was difficult. I fantasized about flying to southern Utah and looking for April. But that's all it was—fantasy. As creative as I was, I couldn't wrap my mind around the ethics of the situation, let alone the practical problems. How do you find someone in a polygamist colony?

I told my mother about April.

"Time will heal," she said. "Time will heal."

My last night in Denver we had a family dinner at Mataam Fez, an authentic Moroccan restaurant on Colfax where you sit on the floor and eat with your fingers. (After I left Colorado, my father had dropped Giuseppe's from his favorites list.)

On December 30, I flew from Denver to Chicago and stayed in the Monaco Hotel just a block from the Leo Burnett Building until I could find an apartment. Mr. Ferrell arrived that evening, and on New Year's Eve we began the first of our meetings with the CEO of Leo Burnett Chicago, Mr. Edward Grant.

Mr. Grant was, of course, aware of the work we had done in New York and was eager to get the Chicago team plugged into our program. Being New Year's, the agency closed at noon, so after just two hours, we began winding down so we could introduce Mr. Ferrell to the creative teams. As we were getting ready to leave Mr. Grant's office, he asked why I had left Chicago. I told him the truth. When I finished, Mr. Grant paged his assistant. "Get me Holly in H.R."

Shortly after our meeting I went down to visit the creative directors on their individual floors, leaving Mr. Ferrell and Mr. Grant behind. I stopped in the energy room for some popcorn, then went to see Kim in front of Potts's office. She was working intently on her computer and didn't notice me standing at her desk.

"I thought they would have let you out on good behavior by now," I said.

Kim's face was animated with excitement. "J.J.!" She jumped up and came around her desk to hug me. "What are you doing here?"

"Just visiting the old neighborhood."

"It's so good to see you. How is New York?"

"New York *was* . . ." I paused to find the right word. "Interesting. But I've been transferred again. I'm back in Chicago."

Kim was so excited she hugged me again. "I'm so happy for you. This is so exciting."

"What's so exciting?" Potts asked, walking from his office. I turned to face him.

"I think she means I am, Peter."

He froze at the sight of me. "What are you doing here?"

"I'm coming back."

"Not on my watch you're not. I don't know how you got here, but I guarantee you won't last here more than a week."

He didn't see Mr. Grant and Mr. Ferrell walk up to us. "Never guarantee what you can't deliver, Peter," Mr. Grant said, his voice angry but controlled.

"Mr. Grant . . ." Potts said. Then he turned to Mr. Ferrell, genuflecting. "Mr. Ferrell, it is such an honor to meet you. Your work, the Florence Initiative, is sheer genius."

"You should tell that to the man who made it happen," he said, turning to me. "I believe you've met Mr. Jacobson, our new Global Chief Creative Officer for Leo Burnett Worldwide."

Potts looked like a man who had just been convicted of double homicide.

"Unfortunately," Mr. Ferrell said, "from what I just heard, it sounds like you have a problem working with him."

Potts flushed. "No. Not at all. Things are good," he said, turning to me. "Everything's good, right?"

"Not everything," Mr. Grant said. "As you know, Peter, Leo Burnett is proud of the work we've done in creating an egalitarian work environment. We've worked hard to abolish the traditional models of corporate hierarchy and elitism and replaced it with cooperation and teamwork.

"I just spoke with H.R. It would seem that our way of doing business is very much at odds with your practice of what I'll call for lack of a better term, *personnel exiling*. For that reason we'll be making some changes. Timothy Ishmael will be your replacement as senior creative director."

Peter looked panicked. "Please don't fire me."

"We're not firing you," Mr. Grant said. "We have a wonderful opportunity for you in New York. In fact, it's the very same opportunity you gave Mr. Jacobson, and look how that worked out for him." He winked at me. "And I'm told that you've already met your new manager, Leonard Sykes."

I finally understood the dream I'd had in New York. And Leonard's broken pots.

# CHAPTER

## Thirty-two

*I have decided to journey the dark path to my past—to find the light of hope or to permanently extinguish it.*

✦ Joseph Jacobson's Diary ✦

At noon the agency closed. I took my things to the hotel, then caught the Blue Line at Clark and Lake. I was going to the diner. A small, hopelessly optimistic part of my psyche hoped that April might have called and left some contact information with Ewa or one of the waitresses. But the realist in me knew that wasn't likely. I was going to the diner to formalize my loss and put the past to rest—like going to a funeral to see the deceased.

I had intended to go straight to Mr. G's, but when the train stopped at Irving Park, my breath caught a little. How many times had my heart ached as she stepped off the train here to go home? Then I thought of something. Perhaps April's roommate, Ruth, would know how to find her. I jumped off the train just before the doors closed.

In spite of the patches of ice, I practically ran the distance to her apartment. The main-level door was locked, so I buzzed the apartment, twice, but there was no answer. I waited there a few minutes until a tenant walked up to the door and opened it. I slipped in after her and went up the stairs to April's apartment. There was a FOR RENT sign on the door. I don't know why I was so surprised. April had been gone for nearly two years. I never should have gotten my hopes up.

I walked back to the platform, taking the next train just two stops west to the Jefferson Park station. It took me fifteen minutes to walk from the station to my old apartment.

It was a little past three in the afternoon. The traffic along Lawrence was light, the street dusted in white, its curbs concealed beneath tall banks of dirty snow. Even though it was freezing cold, across the street from my old apartment a woman in a parka was sitting on the steps of her house blowing soap bubbles for her dog.

I couldn't believe that I'd ever lived in that place. Already it seemed like a lifetime ago. I wondered if this was how soldiers felt returning to a battlefield in peacetime.

I remembered. That first sleepless night walking down Lawrence Avenue, first to the Polish market, then, later that same night, to the diner. The night I met *her*.

Oftentimes it's the smallest, seemingly inconsequential acts that make the biggest differences in our lives. What if April had remembered to lock the door at closing time? How different my life would be. How different I would feel at this moment. It was so easy falling in love with her. Why couldn't letting her go be just as easy?

I took a picture of the ugly apartment building with my phone, then headed further down Lawrence toward the diner.

At the sight of Mr. G's the memories flooded back, carrying such joy and pain with them I didn't know if I could hold them all. *Maybe this wasn't such a good idea after all*, I thought.

No, it wasn't an easy thing to do, but it was the right thing to do. There was no sense prolonging the agony. It was time to face the corpse of my failure, shut the lid on it and move on.

Even though they were open for New Year's Eve, the diner was nearly empty. It was that slow hour—too late for lunch, too early for dinner. Everything looked the same as before. I sat down at a booth and picked up a menu, even though I already knew everything on it. Nothing had changed. Not even the daily special.

No, *everything* had changed.

"May I help you?" I looked up to see Ewa standing above me. "Hey, long time no see," she said awkwardly as if she'd just learned the phrase.

"It's good to see you, Ewa."

"It is good to be seen," she said. "How have you been?"

"Surviving," I said.

"That is better than not."

"Usually," I said. I took a deep breath. "You haven't heard from April, have you?"

She looked at me as if she didn't understand my question. "Haven't heard?"

"I mean, has she called?"

"Yes."

"How is she?"

"She is okay, I think. She could be better, but okay."

"Is she happy?"

Her brow furrowed. "That is a very difficult question to answer. Maybe you should ask her for yourself." Ewa turned back toward the counter. I looked over. April was standing there, staring at me.

"April." I jumped to my feet and walked to her, our eyes locked on each other. I couldn't read her. I didn't know what she was thinking.

We stood there, just inches from each other. Maybe miles. I wasn't sure. "I never meant to lose you," I said.

Tears began to well up in her eyes.

"I came back to find you . . . but you were gone. Then they sent me to New York." I wanted to touch her—to throw my arms around her. "I never stopped thinking about you." I just looked into her eyes, hoping she would say something. She didn't. "Why did you leave?"

She wiped her eyes. "After what I told you, I thought you had left me. It was too much for me. You're the first man I've ever truly chosen. At Christmas, I called Ewa to wish her Merry Christmas. She told me you had come for me. So I called, but your phone was turned off. So I came back. I went to your apartment . . ." She paused. "But you were gone." She wiped her eyes. "I didn't know a heart could break twice."

"I'm so sorry." My voice cracked. "I was so stupid. I scared you away."

"You didn't scare me away," she said. "I needed to go back. I needed to take care of my past, so I could have a future."

I stood there, still frozen, afraid to ask. "Am I a part of that future?"

She looked into my eyes with a peculiar light, then slowly shook her head. "No."

My heart fell. "No?"

"Not just a part," she said. "I was hoping you would be my future."

She fell into me and we kissed. Passionately. Fully. This time there was no past to suppress, no secrets to steal her away, no guilt to own her. This time, for the first time, she was mine. I would never let her go again.

# EPILOGUE

*Life's greatest lessons are often those we most wished to avoid.*

.✶.Joseph Jacobson's Diary .✶.

The day I graduated from college my father gave me this letter.

*My Dear Son,*

*I am so very proud of you. Now, as you prepare to embark on a new journey, I'd like to share this one piece of advice. Always, always remember that—*

*Adversity is not a detour. It is part of the path.*

*You will encounter obstacles. You will make mistakes. Be grateful for both. Your obstacles and mistakes will be your greatest teachers. And the only way to not make mistakes in this life is to do nothing, which is the biggest mistake of all.*

*Your challenges, if you'll let them, will become your greatest allies. Mountains can crush or raise you, depending on which side of the mountain you choose to stand on. All history bears out that the great, those who have changed the world, have all suffered great challenges. And, more times than not, it's precisely those challenges that, in God's time, lead to triumph.*

*Abhor victimhood. Denounce entitlement. Neither are gifts,*

rather cages to damn the soul. Everyone who has walked this
earth is a victim of injustice. Everyone.

    Most of all, do not be too quick to denounce your sufferings.
The difficult road you are called to walk may, in fact, be your
only path to success.

I've read that letter many times throughout my life. I never
could have imagined how prophetic my father's words would
prove—especially the last line. Had it not been for the difficult circumstances I was thrown into, I never would have
been in the position to ultimately save those I cared most
deeply about. I never would have found my true soul. And I
never would have found *her*. A philosopher once wrote that
we "understand our lives looking backward, but we must live
them forward." He was right. Looking back, the journey all
makes sense. At the time, none of it did.

I am indeed a blessed man. April and I were married in June,
six months after our reunion. If I had to go through all I did
just to have her, I would. In a heartbeat.

    My father is now officially retired, and he and Mom are
traveling the world. They've made a goal to see every country. I'm sure they'll accomplish it. My father never fails at
what he sets out to do. What a legacy he's left his children.

    The Leo Burnett/Jacobson Advertising Agency is thriving.
It's now the largest agency in Colorado. Rupert is the acting
CEO. I'm proud of my big brother. My own career is doing

well. Mr. Ferrell has been good to me. Advertising has been good to me. Chicago's a nice place to live. Maybe someday the Cubs will win the pennant. I'm not holding my breath. There might be something to that goat curse.

One more thing. April and I are going to be parents. She's due next October. If it's a girl, we're thinking of naming her May.

*R*ichard Paul Evans is the #1 bestselling author of *The Christmas Box*. Each of his twenty-one novels has been a *New York Times* bestseller. There are more than 15 million copies of his books in print worldwide, translated into more than twenty-four languages. He is the recipient of numerous awards, including the American Mothers Book Award, the *Romantic Times* Best Women's Novel of the Year Award, the German Audience Gold Award for Romance, two Religion Communicators Council Wilbur Awards, the *Washington Times* Humanitarian of the Century Award and the Volunteers of America National Empathy Award. He lives in Salt Lake City, Utah, with his wife, Keri, and their five children. You can learn more about Richard on Facebook at www.facebook.com/RPEfans, or visit his website, www.richardpaulevans.com.

Also by *New York Times* bestselling author
# Richard Paul Evans:
## The Walk series

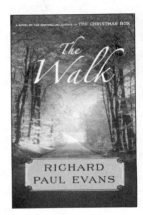
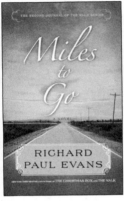
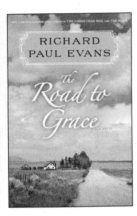

What would you do if you lost everything—your job, your
home, and the love of your life—all at the same time?
When it happens to Alan Christoffersen, he leaves behind
all that he's known in search of hope. What he finds
on his journey will save his life and inspire yours.

**"Hoda and I both thoroughly enjoyed this book....**
**The Walk is beautifully written."**
–Kathy Lee Gifford, host of the *Today* show

Available wherever books are sold or at SimonandSchuster.com

# Are you missing out?
# Join Richard Paul Evans on Richard's Facebook Author Page.

Richard himself contributes almost daily.

Richard's page has fun facts, great contests, first peeks, deep thoughts, GratiTuesday, and just about everything you want to know about one of America's most beloved authors. When you join this thriving community you'll get to know Richard like you never dreamed possible. Join us today!

It's easy to join.
1. Login to Facebook
2. Search www.facebook.com/RPEfans
3. Click on LIKE. Welcome!

Or write to him at P.O. Box 712137
Salt Lake City, Utah 84171